GOD
DOESN'T MAKE
MISTAKES

Recia McLeod Edmonson

WESTBOW
PRESS®
A DIVISION OF THOMAS NELSON
& ZONDERVAN

WestBow Press books may be ordered through booksellers or by contacting:

WestBow Press
A Division of Thomas Nelson & Zondervan
1663 Liberty Drive
Bloomington, IN 47403
www.westbowpress.com
1 (866) 928-1240

Because of the dynamic nature of the Internet, any web addresses or links contained in this book may have changed since publication and may no longer be valid. The views expressed in this work are solely those of the author and do not necessarily reflect the views of the publisher, and the publisher hereby disclaims any responsibility for them.

Any people depicted in stock imagery provided by Getty Images are models, and such images are being used for illustrative purposes only. Certain stock imagery © Getty Images.

Scripture taken from the King James Version of the Bible.

ISBN: 978-1-6642-0043-2 (sc)
ISBN: 978-1-6642-0068-5 (e)

Print information available on the last page.

WestBow Press rev. date: 08/19/2020

CONTENTS

FOREWORD

I wrote this book in 1990, and then my writing was interrupted as I finished my degree and became a teacher for sixteen years. During that time I edited it once in 1994. During those 16 years I first lost my older brother, my Mother, an uncle, a couple of brothers-in-law, and then my beloved husband started his battle with cancer, through that time we became closer than we ever were. We found our faith in God became stronger. I lost my brother two months before my husband passed in 2014.

My greatest and most special memory was the last devotion that we shared. His request was for me to read John chapter 14, mainly because it was his favorite, but I believe somehow, he knew that this was his last day on earth. After I read the chapter he asked me to read the first three verses again "John 14:1-3 (KJV) *14 Let not your heart be troubled: ye believe in God, believe also in me.² In my Father's house are many mansions: if it were not so, I would have told you. I go to prepare a place for you. ³ And if I go and prepare a place for you, I will come again, and receive you unto myself; that where I am, there ye may be also.* And then the sixth verse ⁶ *Jesus saith unto him, I am the way, the truth, and the life: no man cometh unto the Father, but by me.*" After that he reached for my hand and as I held his hand he said "You need to rest, honey. Me and God-we have this under control. I love you. And remember that God doesn't make mistakes." That very night he moved on to heaven.

Although this is a fictional work, I placed in it many real scriptures and spiritual truths. In this work I seek only to honor and glorify my Lord and Savior. Christ alone will always guide your paths if you let

Him in. First of all give your heart and life to Jesus. It is my prayer that if you do not have Jesus as your Savior you will ask Him to come into your heart today. I hope you enjoy the book, but most of all I pray that you find God through it. God's Word will help you through these times. Start reading His Words today.

Sincerely, Recia McLeod Edmonson

DEDICATION

I dedicate this book to my children, Alice, Andrea, and Davie, who have supported my efforts, they were there for me in the loss of their father, and have lovingly taken care of me on my journey without him.

I also dedicate this book to my best friend-my sister, Sue who is my source of confidence. She has believed in me, prayed for me, and encouraged me.

CHAPTER
ONE

Emily watched streams of pink and orange blend as they made brilliant patterns of light on the pale grey curtain of the brand new day. As the once darkened sky gave way to the morning sunlight, she felt her heart rise in the elation of the day's beginning. This was her special t quiet time to spend with God, "Oh Lord the morning sunrise is so beautiful. Thank you so much for this new day and the ability to enjoy this time with You". After reading the word and communing with her Savior she always loved watching the new day begin.

As the sunlight gave birth to the vivid morning sky, she felt at peace and her thoughts gave way to the events of the past that had led to the way her life was today. "If I had known then what I know now, would I change the decisions that I made? Would I want to change anything about my life up to this point? What would I have done in a different way?"

She began to think back to everything that had happened in her life. Making the choice to move was a difficult decision. Although there had been good times, there was so much pain and sadness as well. Emily was a beautiful, tiny petite young woman with brown eyes, framed by long thick eyelashes and long dark black hair, when the life changes began. The memories were permanently engraved in her mind. Life changing moments brought a brand new situation, but she knew that she was comfortable with those changes. Her faith in God was stronger and regardless of everything, God had brought her through it all.

In spite of the unhappiness she had endured, there was joy in the new life that she had and the people who were a part of that life now. Closing her eyes she was transported to the day that led to the point of all the changes in her life. As she sat enjoying her coffee at the beginning of this new day, she was remembered the day it all began. She found herself viewing each detail of the past. It seemed that it had only been a short time that she and Alex had lived on the edge, as they lived from paycheck to paycheck. Often she wondered if they would make it, but God always helped. Any unforeseen bill or doctor bill sent them scrambling to see from where the money would come.

They always tried to remember to put God first. When they returned to Him what was His first, God always blessed them. They also learned an important lesson as they developed their walk with the Lord. On those rare occasions when they had failed to put God first, hard times came. Those times they learned the importance of always choosing to put God first in all things. Most people would find these hardships causing problems in their marriages, but with God at their center, she and Alex grew closer and stronger. When her faith wavered, Alex always knew just what to do and when his faith grew strained they both prayed and read their Bibles a little more.

In the lean times, her children seemed to understand-most of the time. There had been times when they questioned, but Alex took his role as head of the family seriously and took them aside to counsel and pray with them. Emily smiled as she thought about her girls as little children. Not being able to give her children things other children took for granted often hurt Emily, but she knew that they had always provided warmth, food, and love. God always provides for us. He never said that He would give us what we wanted, but what we needed. Often she cried because it hurt her, but at the same time she never let her tears be seen to show strength to her girls. Her faith in God is what always saw her through, because she knew that one day Jesus would return and set up His kingdom and all who believed and accepted Him would live in peace forever. God and God alone would make all things right.

Emily closed her eyes and thought about her girls. They were grown now but it seemed only yesterday they were little girls. Leigha, her oldest daughter, was blonde with light grey blue eyes like Alex's. Although she often wanted her way, Emily knew that she was not a selfish child. She dreamed about becoming rich so she could have a horse. Horses and basically all animals brought her joy. Leigha seemed to have a natural way with animals. Although they only had a small acre of land at one time or the other, it had been a home to dogs, cats, rabbits, chickens, turkeys, two doves, a pheasant, and even a pot belly pig. Emily smiled as she thought about the way all of her girls loved animals. Emily always wished she could get Leigha a horse, but never thought that it would ever be possible.

Nancy, her second child, had sparkling green eyes that complemented her dark auburn hair. She was a bit shy but everyone that ever made friends with her loved her. Nancy was artistic in drawing, painting and crafts and when she was young, Emily taught her needle point and cake decorating and of course she excelled in both – better than Emily was. Nancy had the love of reading and books. Her analytical mind often showed in the decisions that she made. Even as a child she always displayed a hunger for learning.

Ariel, Emily's youngest daughter, had dark hair like Emily but grey eyes like Alex. She was quiet and soft spoken. Ariel liked house work and had followed Emily around since she was little. It was obvious that she felt more comfortable in the house. Often Ariel would listen quietly to others talking and it seemed like she had to think things through before asking questions about what she didn't understand. It was not unusual for her to ask a question out of the blue. Ariel's ability to observe things was uncanny. Emily remembered an occasion when they had gone to a restaurant to eat. After that trip on the way home Ariel began telling about some of the people she had seen. Describing accurate details even down to the shoes they wore. Emily thought about the girls likes and dislikes from those early years and how their personalities had developed and changed over the years.

As she was reminiscing over the past her thoughts turned to Alex. A warm feeling filled her soul. Alex was extremely handsome with brown hair and blue grey eyes. His large frame came from years of hard work not from working out in some gym, which he called the lazy way of getting fit. His eyes were the first thing Emily had noticed. It seemed he could look straight into your soul. As the years went by she realized that his eye color changed with his mood. When Alex became angry they were a sharp blue and when he was worried they were grey. They were a glassy blue when he was experiencing sorrow.

Alex was an optimist and faced life cheerfully. He was a wonderful husband, friend, father and lover. Although he was kind and gentle, but his expressions often made people think he was cold and stern. Those looks led people to fail to see his softer side. His laughter was contagious when he allowed someone to see it. Alex would always have a special place in her heart. Emily was short and tiny and always felt safe when he wrapped his strong arms around her. Alex often joked as he enfolded her into his arms, "Come to my cocoon my little butterfly."

Emily thought back to when she first became aware of Alex, actually he had taken her and her friend Donna to the fair once when she was younger. Alex lived next door to Emily and she had watched him many times as he worked on his car or did yard work. He was older and so she basically had a huge crush on him. Later she had dated a high school boy named Curtis, but that didn't work out, one day Alex came over to her yard after she broke up with Curtis. That was the first time she had talked to him. He joined the Navy and was gone for four years. Soon after he returned from the Navy, Emily went to her best friend Donna's house and Donna introduced her to Alex, although Donna knew that he was Emily's neighbor. Donna knew the two of them had never really talked. Later as she spent more time at Donna's house, she found that Alex was a regular visitor. As Emily and Alex talked together they got to know each other. It seemed that he was always there, but she had no idea why. Then one day when she and Donna were on their way to town, Donna told her that her uncle wanted to date her.

"How does your uncle know me and how old is he anyway?" Emily inquired.

Donna laughed, "Silly, it's Alex and you have been talking to him for about six months now!"

Emily stared at her and replied, "Alex is your uncle? I thought he was a friend of the family."

Donna told her, "Because he is a few years older than you are, he doesn't think you would go out with him." Emily nodded her head to tell Donna, "I am... already interested."

It was just a little while later that Alex asked her to go to the movies. That was how it all began. They both knew almost immediately that there was definitely chemistry between them. Six months later they were married. Alex always joked around that he saw what he wanted and went after it.

With each hardship they faced their relationship grew stronger as they relied on God to see them through. After the loss of a child, their marriage as well as their faith was tested. Alex stood firm in his belief that God didn't make mistakes and she could almost hear him now. He would look into her brown eyes with his blue grey eyes and say, "Em, God doesn't make mistakes and He always knows exactly what He is doing. We just need to trust Him at all times."

The vivid memories of Alex and the girls changed as her mind flowed back to the day when everything had changed. Her mind filled now with the vision of the three strangers that came to her door. From that moment everything started happening so fast. She leaned back in her swing and closed her eyes as her mind focused on the past....

Emily heard the car outside and went to the window and peeked out as a big black SUV pulled into the driveway. Two men and a woman exited and walked up the sidewalk. They were all dressed in business suits and Emily was thinking, "Great sales people in threes!" As she opened the door, she noticed carefully how each one appeared. The first man to speak wore a blue suit carefully matched shirt and tie. He had a wide smile and dark thinning hair with a bit of grey at the temples. The second man was shorter with sandy hair and a bald spot on top. He was dressed in a brown suit and smiled pleasantly as well. Both men had a comforting attitude. A woman stood behind them and wore a dark navy pinstriped suit. Her dark hair was pulled back sternly from her face with in a tight bun at the nape of her neck; she wore dark rimmed glasses and was frowning very unhappily with a look of distain as she viewed the house. Emily chose to leave the locked screen door closed as she observed the visitors standing on the front stoop.

"Hello, I am David Sommers." The blue suit guy spoke first. "This is Richard Palmer and Leeann Davis."

"If you are selling something, you are at the wrong house. I can't buy anything no matter what plans you may present. This would just be a waste of your time." Emily smiled and started to close the door. Then as the man in the blue suit handed her a business card she stepped out onto the front porch to accept it. Immediately the words Attorney caught her eye. Sensing her nervousness the man in the brown suit, Mr. Palmer in a thick Australian accent explained, "We represent Mr. Jarrod Newton McLeod."

As soon as he finished the woman chimed in, looking at the little house with disgust, "Are you both sure this is the right house?" This woman's attitude did nothing to alleviate Emily's distrust. In a stern unexpressive way, the rude woman asked, "Mrs. Emily Daniels, is the name Jarrod McLeod at all familiar to you?"

"Yes, McLeod is my maiden name. My father has often spoken of his Uncle Jarod that lives in Australia. What is this and why are you questioning me as if I have done something wrong?" Emily looked straight at the woman, who frowned back at her.

Mr. Sommers, blue suit guy, "We would like to sit down and explain everything to you if we may?"

Emily was uneasy about asking three strangers to enter her house and she pointed at the church across the street, "My father's office is right there, would it be okay if you spoke to me there?"

"Oh yes definitely," Mr. Palmer spoke up. "I was a close friend of Mr. McLeod and he thought very highly of your father and kept a picture of his nephew, Samuel on his desk."

Emily not really sure of what to make of these people, closed her door and they all headed across the church parking lot and entered a side door. As she entered into her father's office, his secretary Dee brightly, smiling shook her head and said, "You have been reading minds again! Your dad just asked me to call you."

Emily laughed and said, "No, Dee, not this time; these people and I would like to see Dad for a few minutes. I hope he isn't busy."

"Well, you may not have read my mind this time, but somehow I think that the Lord always seems to know just when to let you know things!" Dee buzzed Emily's Dad and then motioned the group to enter.

The group entered the office; her father a nice looking silver-gray haired man extended his hand and introduced himself, "I am Samuel Dwight McLeod, the pastor here at Immanuel Baptist Church." Emily hugged her Dad and introduced the others. After introductions were made, they all were seated.

Mr. Palmer began speaking, getting right to the point of their visit gave the brief history of her Uncle's past. "Jarrod McLeod was born in Geary, Isle of Skye, Scotland. He immigrated to Australia and became very successful in both his business holdings and in the cattle business. He never married and when he turned ninety he decided to pick the only child of his favorite nephew to inherit his estate. He left your father a nice sum of money, but everything else is yours Mrs. Daniels."

"This news is very unsettling," Emily's father spoke sadly at the thought of his uncle's death.

"I can assure you that Mr. McLeod was very pleased to find that his estate and holdings would be given to your daughter," Mr. Palmer spoke up.

Emily had not spoken nor had she taken her eyes off of her father's face. She kept thinking that this was all a dream and if she spoke it would all come crumbling down. Watching her reactions Mr. Palmer added, speaking to her father, "Your uncle often spoke of your visit to him. It was something he held dear and always told stories about the time that you came to visit. It meant a great deal to him and he never forgot."

"When did he die," Samuel asked. "I used to write him but in the last few years we have lost touch. If I had known that he was ill I would have visited him."

"He died a few months ago, at 100 years old. He had commented that he felt tired and went to bed early. We found him the next morning, holding his Bible. He had a very peaceful smile on his face. Now he is with the Lord and will never be tired again." Mr. Palmer smiled lovingly and it was obvious that he felt a great fondness for her Uncle Jarrod.

Her father spoke looking lovingly at Emily said, "It looks like your Uncle Jarrod has taken care of you and your prayers have been answered."

"I can't believe this and I still think I am dreaming." As Emily was speaking, the woman cleared her throat and very sternly let them know that she had something else to say.

"There is however, one very important condition that must be met in order for you to inherit the entire estate." And with an air of importance and seemingly enjoyment at the news she was to convey, "You have to move to Australia and run the cattle ranch as well as the other aspects of Mr. McLeod's business for ten years before inheriting anything at all." With that bit of information this woman sat back and with a condescending smile.

Mr. Palmer glared at Ms. Davis and it was clear that he did not agree with her methods. He then began to explain, "Emily, I can see the distress on your face, and I assure you that your uncle has set aside money to provide for your family and to run the ranch and the business. You see your uncle loved the ranch and his holdings and wanted to give you an opportunity to see if you would love it too. Mr. McLeod hated the idea of selling the place."

Mr. Sommers added, "You will be trained in taking care of the business and the ranch. The salaries of the employees have been arranged and Mr. Palmer will be there to help you as well."

"Just how much money is this? I don't want my daughter to end up in another country where I can't help her if she needs me." Her father inquired.

"Samuel, May I call you that? Here are some papers to explain things. We can go over them together." Mr. Sommers added.

"Samuel, you will have two million now as your part of the inheritance without any strings attached." Mr. Palmer shot a stern look at Ms. Davis as she sat up straight and started to speak. "Emily your part now is ten million and after the ten years you will receive the bulk of the estate which as of now is one billion. If you learn how to invest and have the touch that your uncle had with money you can easily increase that amount over time."

Emily in shock sat back in her chair and just looked at everyone. Thinking what this day had brought to her. "I cannot believe this is really happening." She looked at her father for assurance.

Ms. Davis almost hatefully added, "Looks like you've been handed gold on a silver platter."

"Oh Dad, what price will I have to pay for this?" Emily searched her father's face for an answer.

"Well, for one you have to move. This is a very important decision and you, Alex and the girls need to talk first." Her Dad hugged her assuredly.

Ms. Davis coldly interjected, "Are you willing to meet the requirements of the will?"

Mr. Palmer and Mr. Sommers shot her an icy stare as she continued almost gleefully, "We have to know by today."

"Oh, Dad! I need to call Alex and get the girls," Emily turned to face the others, "Can we still come home for vacations?"

"Of course you can!" Mr. Palmer added, "Your uncle never intended to shut you away from your family and friends. You can even bring your parents with you if you want."

"That would not be possible at this time for me since I am the pastor of the church here." Her dad said.

"I need to talk to Alex and get the girls," Emily was clearly excited and rattled at the same time. "Daddy, where do I start!"

"Just settle down and take a breath. I will call Alex and you go get the girls." Her father laughed. "I assume, it is okay if she discusses this with her family first."

The others nodded, "I am sorry Emily but we will need an answer by five this afternoon." Mr. Palmer apologized. "We will return this evening for your decision."

Emily shut the door behind them as the lawyers left and turned to her father. He was a tall handsome man, in early sixties with a very deep but pleasing voice. He looked younger in spite of his silver gray hair. "I can't believe this Dad."

"Just relax and always ask God what He wants you to do." Her father said. "I know that you and Alex will make the right decision. But remember that God will bless you as long as you seek His will first."

"Now I can help you for a change. It feels good to be able to say that." She beamed.

Her father smiled, "Now you know my secret. It is why I always loved helping you. I want you to be happy."

"I guess God is answering my prayers, but He actually overdid it a bit."

"Just let God lead and He will keep you safe!" Her father reminded her.

"I know that God will always guide my path. But I have the feeling that my life is about to drastically change. I hope I am ready for this."

"Just trust in the Lord, Em, He will always see you through. Just keep yourself close to Him and He will lead." He repeated his advice hoping it would sink in and calm her.

"Thanks Dad for raising me to believe in Christ and showing me how to always follow Christ's will for my life. I love you Dad."

"I love you, too."

She and her father kneeled in prayer and then Emily left to go get the girls at school as her father called Alex. 'What a day this has been she thought. Now I can help Dad for a change!'

As she left the office and headed for home, Emily felt her first premonition that her life was about to change in a major way. Of course things would change if the family moved and inherited all the money, but Emily knew somewhere deep inside that the changes were to be separate from the money or move; changes that would be more than just a few minor adjustments.

This day was the beginning of everything that had happened to her family. Now as she sat here reminiscing over the past she felt content so she continued to remember her past.

"Mom, why did you pick us up early?" Leigha asked as she got in the car. Nancy and Ariel echoed her question. "Is anything wrong? Mom are you okay:" Nancy worriedly inquired.

"Everything is fine girls, but I have to wait until your father gets home to tell you. So try to be patient." Emily smiled to let them know things were fine. As she sat waiting with the girls for Alex to arrive, thoughts of her family raced through her mind. Alex's strong muscular features stood out in her mind as she picked up a photo frame from the coffee table. There they stood with the girls. He was tall, muscular, and handsome with a strong jaw line and intriguing smile. He was her reason for happiness. In the beginning, his feelings had been so insecure about her love by often asking her why she loved him so much. However his almost shy attitude towards serious conversations seemed to lead him to use humor to lighten a profound conversation. Sometimes he almost had the qualities of a little boy full of mischief. Smiling at her memory she replaced the photo on the table and walked over to open the front door, then sat down on the sofa. Alex and Emily had achieved that oneness of spirit with each other. She wasn't sure how but they had something that many couples tried to find, but often never found. Her friends commented on more than one occasion that it was really weird how the two of them always seemed to know what the other one was thinking and doing.

The girls were a lot like him. They loved to joke around and have a good time. They laughed a great deal of the time-except when they were fussing of course. Emily smiled as she felt so lucky to be blessed by God with such a beautiful family. Leigha, her oldest daughter, had a lot of friends and was very outgoing. She was involved in many school activities. Nancy her second daughter was shy but still had many friends but she enjoyed a more constant routine. Although she was active in school, she liked things ordered and structured with little change. Even though she loved structure she had never been hard to please. Ariel her youngest daughter was even more different in that she always held her opinions until she had examined every detail. Details, the word made Emily smile, Ariel had always been the one who noticed every little detail about her surroundings. Even small details that no one noticed were not undiscovered by her eagle eye.

Thinking about her children brought to mind the news that she would soon share with her family. She wondered how they would react. She still wasn't sure of her own feelings about what was about to transpire. She sat silently wondering about what it meant to be rich. What would it mean and what price would it cost to her and her family? An uneasy premonition filled her with a sense of dread. Can this much really be a good thing? What if it causes me to lose my family or my faith? She silently prayed for God's guidance in everything that was to come.

Suddenly the door opened and the girls came running in from their bedroom to greet Alex as he entered. Everyone speaking at once until Alex held up his hand for them to be quiet and sit down, "Okay, now Emily, Grandpa wouldn't say why, just that I needed to hurry. What's going on? He assured me that everyone was okay and that you would tell us when we were all together."

Taking a deep breath, Emily started telling them her news, "To begin I am fine and we have an extremely important decision to make. So everyone gather around the table and I will tell you the news I have received today."

As everyone assembled in the dining room with Alex at the head of the table, Emily began. She repeated the story of the money and the conditions that were laid out by the lawyers. "We will have to move if we accept. The reason for the hurry is that they need my answer by 5:00 o'clock today. I wanted plenty of time to discuss this and pray with you all about it."

At first they all sat quietly just staring and not knowing what to say or where to begin, they were just as shocked by the news as Emily was.

Leigha spoke up first, "Money is good."

Then Nancy, "But I don't want to move."

Next Alex spoke, "It would be nice to not have to worry about finances for a change. I don't want to influence the decisions we make, but I need to tell you the news I received at work this morning." Pausing for a moment before continuing, "You know that there has been a rumor about a major shut down at the plant. I know we have been through lay-offs before, but this morning we were told that Reymus Industry is being bought out by another company and no one's job is secure. We may or may not be hired by the new company." Pausing briefly then continuing, "I could be jobless by the end of this month or even tomorrow...your news Emily could be an answer to my prayers."

Emily reminded them, "We will be very far away from everyone we know and love."

"Well you know we could afford to visit often." Alex grinned trying to lighten the mood.

Leigha, who sometimes came across as selfish, showed that she really wasn't added, "Mom it would be nice not to see that worried and disappointed look on your face when you can't buy us things." Emily smiled as she always knew Leigha had a tender loving side.

Nancy with her intellect and artistic eye spoke up, "It might be a good adventure. I have seen pictures of Australia and we just might like it there...although I will miss my friends and I am scared of trying a new school." Emily smiled at her pretty daughter who was always the first to understand. She often understood when no one else did. This is why she was loved so much by her friends and family.

Alex looked at Ariel who sat quietly observing everyone and inquired, "What about it Ariel? What do you want to do?" Emily knew that Ariel would weigh everything and probably in a couple of weeks tell her true feelings.

Ariel shrugging her shoulders spoke, "It is alright with me if we go or if we stay that's okay too...but if the new house is bigger can I have my own room?"

Everyone laughed and Alex patted Ariel on the head, "Of course, you girls have been cramped into one room way too long."

"Now everyone join hands," Alex requested. "We must bow our heads and ask God to guide us so that we make the right decision."

Just as they finished praying, the phone rang and Alex went to answer it. The girls started making plans about what they could do with the money. Emily reminded them that money did not buy happiness. "Happiness comes from God and God alone."

"Well do you think God would care if I have a horse?" Leigha cautiously asked.

Emily smiled and at that moment Alex entered the room and crossed over to Emily and knelt in front of her holding her hands in his, "You have always done without to make ends meet. This family has always come first with you. You have been unselfish in everything you do. Giving sometimes what was meant for you in order for the kids or me could have something."

Emily was a bit uncomfortable being the center of attention, "You know I will always put the family first. So what's your point?"

Alex continued, "That was Carl, my foreman. The plant begins shut down tomorrow. The new owners have decided to dismantle the plant." Alex looked at each face and then at Emily. Taking her chin in his hands, "It's your turn to have things and not have to worry."

Leigha said gleefully, "I think God just told us what to do."

Ariel smiled, "Sometimes God answers right away, Mom."

"That's right Ariel!" Alex patted her on the head.

Nancy stood up and said, "All in favor of moving raise your hand." Everyone raised their hands in agreement.

"Well, I guess I need to call Dad and the lawyers now that we have reached a decision." Emily went into the other room to make the call. Upon returning to the room, Alex lifted her and twirled her around. "Emily, you'll see this is a turning point for us. God doesn't make mistakes. He is in control…and well you will see."

Alex smiled and his happiness was apparent to the whole family as his joy spilled over to infect them all. Emily felt sure that this was God's will but somehow she had an eerie feeling about it. Maybe it was just because everything was happening so fast. Riches were not just money, because they had always been rich in God's love and their own love for each other. Alex leaned down and kissed her, "You will see! God has a purpose and a plan for us."

"Ugh they are at it again!" Leigha and the girls were laughing. The mood changed as they busied themselves with final preparations for their upcoming move. From this point it seemed like everything was in fast motion. The lawyers came and papers were signed and plans were made for their trip. They arranged for correspondence course work for the girls to take to finish their school year and until they settled in to the new lifestyle. Larger furniture and other things that they didn't want sent on were given away to needy families and some others shared with friends. Sentimental items and personal items were shipped to the new home. Their visas, passports, and travel arrangements were finalized. The church gave them a going away party and many tears were shed as they said their goodbyes.

They spent their last day with family. Early the next morning they made their way to the airport, and upon arrival it seemed like all of their friends were there to say goodbye. People were staring and wondering who needed forty-five people to see them off. All Emily could do was cry, as she said goodbye to everyone. As they boarded the plane and found their seats, Alex reached over and wiped a tear from her face, "Better turn off the water works before you flood the plane!" He always knew how to cheer her up. As they taxied down the runway, "Well this is it! No turning back now." Emily commented and turned to look at the girls who were wide eyed as the plane left the runway. They all exclaimed, "Wow."

Although it would be summer here when they left it would be winter in Australia. A long trip was planned with a few stops along the way. They planned to see Disney Land with the girls and then a stop in Hawaii. Mr. Palmer was to stay with them on their journey to see that they received money and help along the way. He made sure that they had the best hotels and food. It was a totally new experience for the family.

One morning just after their morning devotional, she and Alex sat drinking coffee on the balcony of their hotel in Hawaii, "Emily, I can see God's hand in all of this. I know that you have worried about moving, but it's just your uncertainty about change. And this is a big change over what we are used to having. Nancy gets her dislike for change from you. I know that you have prayed for strength and assurance from God…" Alex continued, "I feel God has been in this all along. First you get this news, my job shuts down, then this, and everything was wrapped up so quickly and without a hitch. Now here we are taking the trips we always wished we could afford…of course we won't forget God in any of this. He will always come first and we gave to our church from what money they gave us first. I think as long as we don't forget to keep God in our lives that we will be blessed no matter what else happens…we have each other and most importantly-God." Alex looked into her eyes and smiled, "Even if we didn't have all this we are still blessed. You'll see babe, God has a plan and a purpose for all of this. Why else would an uncle you have never seen remember you? God doesn't make mistakes!" Alex pulled her close and smiled mischievously, "Now that money isn't an issue, wanna' make some new plans." Emily knew that looked and smiled back.

Later that day as she watched the sun set, she read her favorite scripture, Psalm 23. As she reflected on the meaning of the words "He leads me beside still waters…" She reminded herself that God was always with her and would always be with her as she read the last of the Psalm… "Surely goodness and mercy will follow me all the days of my life." She began her prayer, "*Lord I have always tried to leave my life in your hands. Please take my uncertainty away and help me to remember that You are always with me. Help me to always seek your guidance in every step I take that I will always let others see You through my life. Thank you for always being with me and thank you for saving my soul. I love you dear Jesus. Amen*"

Emily went inside and reminded everyone that they had to leave early in the morning so they needed to have devotion and prayers and get into bed.

The next day as the plane left, Emily's uneasy feelings returned and she said a prayer for God to comfort her and protect them. She felt as though they had been on a long vacation and now it was time to go home. Only their new home would be in another country and somewhere she had not ever seen, suddenly she felt like she had boarded the wrong plane and that she needed to get off and go back. At the same time she knew, although she was uncertain that this is where God was leading them to be. She also wondered what the new place would be like and maybe worried a bit about everyone being happy. Looking at Alex, who had fallen peacefully asleep and then watching the girls who were excitedly talking about everything they had experienced these last few days, she remembered that God was with them and would always be with them. As she watched the girls happily talking and Alex sleeping she wondered if they had ever thought about what the new place would be like. Emily settled back and found herself needing rest too. So she closed her eyes and was soon sleeping too.

CHAPTER
TWO

~

On their arrival in Sydney, her fears were erased as they hurried to find their luggage and find a car to take them to their hotel. Mr. Palmer, who had flown ahead from Hawaii, and his wife were there to meet them as they exited the airport. It was so good to see a familiar face in the crowd.

"Hey, it is good to see you, Mr. Palmer." Alex reached out and shook hands with him.

"Oh just call me Richard and this is my wife Catherine."

After introductions were made, they loaded in the waiting van and made their way to the hotel where they would be staying for a few days.

"I doubt seriously that I will ever drive in this city." Emily laughed.

"That is exactly how I feel when I come to the US," Richard smiled.

Everyone's excitement was very clear as Leigha exclaimed, "It is so beautiful here, different, but exciting at the same time." The other girls chimed their agreement. Then Richard started going over their schedule for the time they would spend here.

"You have a four day lay over here in the city, before traveling to your home. We want to show you as much of the city and surrounding area while you are here. I have made arrangements for you to stay at my favorite hotel and Catherine and I will show you the city. My daughter, Breanne is 22, a licensed Nanny will take the girls to show them the areas that will be of interest to them as well as staying with them at night while we investigate the night life here, if that is okay with you. We will be here a few days and then we leave early for Melbourne where we will spend a few more days."

"After all that will we get to see our new house?" Ariel inquired. "I am supposed to get my own room…if it's big enough." She had been relatively quiet while Mr. Palmer read the itinerary, but Emily smiled at her daughter, knowing that she would soon let them all know what she was thinking behind those quiet smiles.

Richard grinned and said, "We just wanted you to see part of your new country first."

"Besides sweetie they are probably getting things ready for this bunch to get to our new place." Alex joked. "If it isn't big enough we will build you a room."

"Well now it looks like we have been found out!" Richard added. "You certainly had us figured out!" Turning to Ariel he grinned and without saying anything about the place he added, "You will have your own room."

Emily looked at Alex and then at Richard, "This man never pulls any punches. When he wants to know something or if he has an opinion out it comes."

"Well I hope you don't mind because the staff had just returned from vacation and needed some extra time to open up and get the house ready."

"We don't mind!" The girls all chimed in. Everyone laughed. "We are having fun."

Emily thought about how much she enjoyed the Palmers and their company had been valued. She only wished the Palmers lived closer to where they would be living. She mentally reprimanded herself trying to remember that this was now their new home. She and Alex rested while Breanne came and took the girls to see some of the sights that the younger children might enjoy.

After the girls left and once she and Alex had rested, Richard and Catherine came to show them the sights of Sydney. The highlight of Emily's day was the water taxi. It was relaxing and a great way to see the sights as they saw the harbor and cruised by the enormous Sydney Opera House. They visited the cove where the first settlers, marines and prisoners planted crops and farmed the land, also the beautiful Royal Botanical Gardens there. Visiting the famous opera house and its unique architecture was exciting. The pictures she had seen in books could not even begin to show how marvelous it was. They ate at a nice restaurant and then went shopping at the biggest mall she had ever seen. It had four levels filled with every kind of store imaginable.

"I could spend a month here and still not see everything!" Emily laughed.

"Well once you two get settled, you can come in to the city and we can shop all day"

Catherine added. "There are a lot more exciting places to shop."

Richard laughed and playfully poked his wife, "Oh yes she is always looking for ways to spend money!"

All in all it was a nice day. Back at the hotel, they rested before the night's adventure. Alex was talking about all the driving rules and regulations. "If we come here we will need to hire a driver." The girls were full of tales of their day the zoo and the aquarium were two of their favorite sites. Breanne was also the topic of conversation, because they loved her. She was certainly good with the girls and seemed to enjoy spending time with them also. After resting that evening Emily and Alex took a harbor dinner cruise with Richard and Catherine. Everything seemed so unreal and Emily kept thinking she would wake up and be back in Arkansas. Watching the lights in the harbor while the cruise lazily coursed through the calm waters, brought a sense of awe to Emily. This would be an experience she would always treasure.

The girls were in bed by the time they returned to the hotel and Emily and Alex cuddled on the sofa for a few minutes before going to bed. Emily smiled up at Alex and traced his jawline with her finger, "This is more than I have ever dreamed! Do you like it here?"

"Yes, I think it's great." He pulled her close. "I can't wait to see our new house. Everything here is extraordinary but exciting . . . kind of like starting over again." Alex noticed her uneasy look, "Are you happy Em? Don't you like it here?"

"Honey, I am happy as long as you are here. I never want to lose you." She looked up at Alex and wondered what her bad feelings had to do with him. Emily laid her head on his massive chest and for a moment she felt secure from all of the dark feelings she had about this move. She suddenly realized that those feelings that had haunted her since this all began did have to do with Alex.

"Em, why are you trembling?" Looking down at her, Alex pulled her closer.

"Oh promise me that you will never leave me. I don't think I could handle ever being without you."

Alex wiped a tear from her eye, "Sweetheart, we have always been close and as long as we keep God in our marriage it will remain strong. Besides I would be crazy to leave such a beautiful... rich lady." He joked as usual when talk gets serious. He teased trying to cheer her up, "Why all this worry when we are finally financially secure."

"I know, it's just one of my feelings that always get stronger when I am with you." She hugged Alex and said, "I get scared thinking about being without you. Will there be a price to pay for all this free money? Is it going to change who we are? Will it make us into something we are not?" Alex brushed her hair from her face and tried to smooth her frown with his finger, "It's the uncertain surroundings and the newness of things. You have never liked change and those feelings probably are stronger with me because you are more relaxed with me. You know that I am here for you." Breaking into his mock Aussie accent, "It's okay mate. No worries." With that he picked her up and said, "Come on my little worry wart." He carried her to bed and there she was safe in his arms and slept soundly.

The days passed quickly, filled with shopping and more sight-seeing while nights were filled with renewing their love and devotion to each other. The family unit was becoming closer as they spent happy carefree hours just enjoying each other's company. Visiting the sights of the city and watching the happy faces of her family made Emily feel secure and happy once more. The whole family was looking forward to seeing the new house and being able to settle into their new life. Emily had a lingering thought that something was too big for Richard to share with them because every time she mentioned their new house, he seemed to always change the subject.

Finally the last day arrived, Emily awakened Alex with a kiss and he drew her close into his arms, "Well we've come a long way from Arkansas little lady." He used his John Wayne accent.

"I can't figure out if I am married to an Australian man or a western American cowboy," Emily teased him.

"I wonder what our new house will be like. Richard says that we will have help with the place. No more lawn mowing!" Alex grinned. "You will have time to write and sew and all the things you like doing. Speaking of writing," he playfully whined and pouted, "You haven't written me a poem in a while. Don't I inspire you anymore?"

Putting on a serious but playful expression, "Well, you are getting pretty old. Not wanting to do yard work anymore. You might get a bit lazy." She playfully pushed Alex. "I will have to trade you in for a younger model and raise him right." Alex pinned her down and began tickling her and at this moment the girls rushed into the room to get in on the fun. The laughter filled the room as the family enjoyed the moment.

This last day in Sydney finally arrived showing signs of being a beautiful day. The excitement was showing on their faces as they began the journey to Melbourne and after their arrival they went to yet another hotel and unpacked. After a brief rest they saw the sights here including the zoo which they loved and took several short trips as well. They saw a town where people were dressed in period costumes and then went to pan for gold. The girls loved this part and did not want to leave. Richard told them they had gold fever. Another side trip was to an island where they got to see penguins. After all the side trips everyone was tired but full of new wonderful memories that would last them for the rest of their lives. Once they left Melbourne and began the last leg of their trip home, they boarded a small passenger plane and Richard in a very matter of fact statement said, "This is your plane and for your use anytime."

Emily shook her head at the enormity of it all and the fact that this money was theirs hit her again. Once they landed and began the last leg of the journey to their estate, the car was unusually quiet as they sat watching the scenery. Emily's mind was on the finality of where the destination would take them.

Alex too felt the enormity of things as Richard told them about the place. "Your property is about 3575 acres and borders the Garrett place which is about 1850 acres. There are several smaller homes on the land, where your ranch hands, farm hands, and house helpers live. We will meet the whole crew later. These families have been employed by your uncle for years. He always has taken great care of them and all of this is figured into his business plans. Alex and Emily you will be shown the ropes to the family business as soon as you are settled."

At that moment a beautiful brick two story house with flowers in the yard came into view. Everyone was watching excitedly, but they drove past it. One of the girls spoke up, "That isn't our house?" "Well that is the foreman's cottage." Richard said.

Ariel quietly but with excitement on her face inquired, "Will our house be that big?"

"Girls there are a lot of surprises for you." Richard smiled.

At that moment they turned into a stone gate and started up another road. Up ahead Emily saw what looked like a small town in the distance with two more nice brick houses on the side; an enormous large brick, three-story house was located in the far center of several out buildings with an extremely large barn off to the rear, directly behind the house. It was a marvelous sight but frightening to Emily at the same time. Fences lined the area and all of a sudden Emily's thoughts were ended as Leigh squealed, "Look, Mom horses."

"They are all yours." Richard laughed.

Alex exclaimed, "Wow look at the size of the house."

Ariel looked overwhelmed, "It will take us all day long to keep it clean."

"I can paint pictures of all the pretty flowers. And it will be fun to take care of them!" Nancy giggled. Her artistic eye had located the obviously beauty of the place.

Emily sat staring at the enormous house and the large front porch with stairs leading up to a huge double entry. The car pulled into a circular drive that led up to the stairs. There was a flower bed with a huge fountain in the middle. Windows with shutters lined the porch on which their little house back home would fit. Richard was explaining that the other houses belonged to Carl and Pam Carlsen, the foreman and his wife, and Larry and Kate Hansen, the gardener and his wife the housekeeper.

Emily looked at Ariel and realized that even though she was excited there was a question in her eyes. No telling what it might be and would probably take a while before she revealed it. Emily had a feeling that Ariel would reserve her comments until she saw inside the house. She would probably want to see if she had her own room first and then she would want to see the kitchen.

"It's quite breathtaking isn't it?" Richard was saying. "I knew that you would like it,"

Alex squeezed Emily's hand and said "It is very big! Well Ariel it looks like you will get your own room."

Ariel asked, "How many other people live here?"

"It all belongs to your family." Richard told her.

"We should have brought Grandma and Grandpa with us." Nancy added.

When Alex looked at Emily she was wiping a tear from her eye. "Hey sweetheart we can still bring them down. Don't be sad."

What he didn't understand was at that moment she realized, along with what Ariel had already expressed, it would be hard to take care of this place. She felt so inadequate in the face of the responsibility she had inherited.

But as if Alex had read her thoughts he said, "Don't cry Em, I never thought or expected all of this either." To Richard he asked, "Why didn't you give us a warning about how big this place is?"

"I have worried ever since I saw how small your place was. I realized it would be a great shock, but Jarrod asked me to keep it a secret so as not to influence your decision. Although since meeting you, I don't believe that it would have done so. If he had been aware of things, I don't think he would have asked that of me. He was just so excited to give the place to you."

"I wish I could have seen him and talked to him. Why didn't he leave it to my Dad?" Emily questioned.

"He knew that your Dad would not leave his church and more than anything he wanted a young couple here. He took great interest in you and finding out all he could. To say that he was excited when he found out about the children would be an understatement."

As they pulled up to the front a very tall rugged but good looking man came out of the house. He had a very smooth deep tan skin. He was smiling and friendly as he opened the door the family exited the car, "This is Larry, your gardener and handyman. Larry this is Emily, Mr. McLeod's great niece, and Alex her husband, and her girls Leigha, Nancy, and Ariel."

They all shook hands and Larry opened the door to the house. As they entered the front foyer the awareness of the new life style filled Emily with wonder. The floors were a polished marble and a large winding staircase led upward to a second floor. The household staff were lined up and ready to be introduced. "This is Kate Hansen, Larry's wife and she is the head housekeeper and cook. These other ladies are Pam, Betty, and Becky. Kate will explain their responsibilities and duties."

"There are many rooms and all kept clean." Kate spoke up and explained and began explaining the duties of each of the ladies. "Pam is in charge of the upstairs, laundry and flower arrangements..." Momentarily Emily tuned her out, not meaning to be rude she snapped back to listen as Kate finished. "They all live on your property and are the wives of the stockmen that work the ranch. Becky who is in charge of the mending and downstairs cleaning along with Betty are sisters and live in one of the smaller cottages."

Emily greeted each lady and smiled but stopped in front of Becky, "Do you sew a lot?"

Becky, a very pretty girl with smooth olive skin and beautiful eyes, smiled, "Yes mam I love to sew. I make most of my own clothes."

"I make most of my own clothes as well. We will have much to talk about." Emily smiled

The door opened and Larry and another man entered carrying their bags. He was introduced as Carl Paulsen the Ranch Foreman. He was blond and stocky built. Larry explained that Carl was also in charge of the stockmen. Alex, Richard, Larry, and Carl along with Pam went upstairs to their rooms.

Kate dismissed the others and then began showing them around the first floor. After a few minutes Emily asked, "Kate, may we wait until later for the rest of the tour? I am exhausted and would like to freshen up and rest a bit. But thank you for everything."

"Of course Mrs. Daniels, I will show you to your room."

Actually Emily's old uneasy feeling had returned. Seeing the place and the wonder of it all left her feeling as if there would be a price to pay for all of this. Somehow she just couldn't accept that it was finally time for her to have so many blessings all at one time.

Alex and the men were coming down the stairs and he took one look at Emily and knew that something was wrong. He wondered about her intuition that had often been spot on, and at times it had both amazed him and scared him too. She was right more often than wrong when she had these premonitions.

Alex went directly to her. "Emily, what's wrong?"

Emily smiled and answered, "I am just very tired and need to rest a bit."

Pam offered to take them to their rooms, but Alex laughed and said he would show her since he now knew the way.

Once in their room Emily crossed over to the window and looked outside. She hadn't even noticed the surroundings of the room. Alex had noticed that she was very pale and withdrawn. "Hey, Babe what's up?" He asked concerned.

"What makes you think something is wrong?" Emily turned around and looked up at her husband.

"I know those dark looks of yours and you are very pale as well. Just say what's churning in that mind of yours."

"Oh Alex I guess I am just very exhausted from all the excitement. Well. . ." after a brief pause she smiled weakly up at her husband, "I get this uneasy feeling and it may be that I just need to rest." Turning to look out the window again, she just sighed.

Alex who always tried to lighten the mood looked around the room and then spoke up, "Just look at the size of this room! We could all fit in here. This is almost half the size of our little house back home."

Turning from the window Emily told him, "That is just it Alex, I have nothing to do here. Everything has already been done. My strange feeling became stronger when we entered the house and I just can't shake it off. Maybe I will feel better after I take a nap."

She crossed over and sat on the bed, looking around the room she smiled weakly at Alex showing that she appreciated the space. Alex knelt beside her and took off her shoes and gently laid her back on the bed. Covering her with a throw blanket, he lay down beside her and held her hand while she drifted off to sleep. He knew she would be better soon.

CHAPTER
THREE

~

After Emily had fallen asleep, Alex quietly exited the room and went down the stairs. He found the girls in the library playing a baby grand piano and singing. Leigha had played the piano since she was five years old. The other girls could play as well, but Leigha was usually the one who played while they sang. Their sweet voices blended well and they enjoyed singing. Singing at church functions and on holidays for the family, had always brought enjoyment to all who heard them.

"Oh Daddy, look at this piano and all the books and sheet music!" Nancy exclaimed.

They were so excited and telling him all about their rooms and Ariel was holding a book from the vast shelves of books. Alex smiled and held up his hands for them stop. "Okay girls, I too am excited about all of this, but I need a cup of coffee."

As he turned to head for the kitchen the girls began singing again. He smiled and walked through a huge dining room toward a door. Opening the door he found the kitchen. The ladies were all preparing the evening meal and Alex crossed over to a small table by a large window and sat down.

Pam came over and asked, "Mr. Daniels is there anything that I can get you, perhaps a cup of tea?"

"Well first of all just call me Alex, please. I am not much of a tea drinker. Don't ya' have some coffee? Good strong and black!"

"Of course, I was expecting that knowing how much Americans love coffee. I just made a fresh pot." Pam went to get the coffee and brought it to him. "You will find we like it too."

As he sipped his coffee, he watched the ladies working. Pam was tall and slender with dark black hair pulled back in a tight bun at the nape of her neck. Betty was slim but shorter than Pam. Becky was a bit on the plump side, but very feisty. She couldn't seem to be still, jumping from one job to another.

The smell of dinner filled the room, "What's for dinner?" Alex asked.

Pam answered, "Roast, potatoes, carrots and all the trimmings. Also we have apple pie for dessert."

Alex waved and smiled, his taste buds were eagerly anticipating the meal. "I can hardly wait! It all smells wonderful."

As he turned to leave, Kate asked, "How is your wife? She really looked pale and we were a little worried."

"She will be fine. We have just had more excitement in the last few weeks than we have had in our whole lifetime. This place was more than any of us expected and when Emily gets overwhelmed she sleeps. Her feelings always seem to get sorted out while she sleeps; I think she talks to God while she sleeps, because she always wakes up refreshed. We would never make it very far without our faith. Do you ladies know the Lord?"

Kate smiled and said, "Oh yes we do and I am so relieved to know that you do too. We weren't sure. We would like to take you to church with us on Sunday."

"That would be great. We were wondering where we would go. Thanks!"

Alex waved and turned to go, but turned back around to face them, "I think this is going to work out just fine. It is great to be here."

They all nodded and waved back at Alex. "It is good to have you here." After Alex left the ladies were all expressing their relief that their new family had faith in Christ.

"I love the girls already. They are so well mannered and did you hear them sing and play?" Pam added.

"I figured they had been to church when I heard them singing hymns." Kate smiled and began humming the tune the girls had been singing.

"I know we all worried and didn't know what to expect with the new owners, but I say God gave us a gift. They all seem like a God fearing family." Becky added.

Emily did awaken refreshed and was back to her old self, but Alex sensed that often she was only putting on a front for all to see. He knew she didn't want anyone to worry about her.

Alex just prayed that God would soon give her peace. He knew he would always worry about her and even though he knew that worry was one of the devil's tools, often he fell prey to it.

As the days advanced Larry and Kate spoiled the girls unmercifully. Ariel was always in the kitchen helping out. Kate had taken her under her wing and was teaching her how to cook. Larry had more or less adopted Leigha and was teaching her about the horses. She rode every day. Becky and Nancy seemed to have the most in common and Nancy would paint and spend time in the garden with the flowers. Nancy also spent time with Emily learning how to sew, often she would go out on the sun porch to draw. Alex adapted to the lifestyle and it seemed he had always done this type of work. He often whistled as he left to go out and work. Emily and the girls spent more quality time together and Emily found that she enjoyed teaching the girls their school lessons. At first she had been unsure of her ability to teach but it was fun for her.

The family found that the church was great and had accepted them. The church was and older building that had been remodeled through the ages. It was originally built in 1828. It was a beautiful building. But just as at home, Emily found that the church was not the building but the people in it. Those people rallied around them from the first Sunday they attended. The girls were soon singing in the choir and before long they began singing specials. It was a good feeling to be with God's people.

The community was a friendly encouraging place. Most of the people were church members and being around them made her feel a part of it. Emily still missed her old friends but she had drawn close to Kate and the others and considered them friends, but she sensed they would always guard their words because they were employees. She longed to meet her nearest neighbors but they were out of the country at the moment. Kate said the people traveled most of the time.

Day to day existence was exciting at first as they explored the vastness of their house. Kate referred to it as the manor. One day on a investigating tour, Alex and Emily opened the basement door and only went a small way into it when Emily stopped and turned around and went out of it. Alex was behind her and she had turned to him and commented, "That place can wait until another day." As usual Alex kidded her about it, but at the same time he decided to visit it later too.

The first floor was mainly the entrance with a huge winding stairway that led to the second floor landing. To one side of the stairway there was a hallway that led to the parlor room, a downstairs bathroom and a library. On the other side of the entry was a doorway to the living room another hallway between the living room and dining room led to the ballroom. The ballroom was large and filled with windows. It was well kept but huge. It had a stage area at the end of it. A large grand piano was on the platform there. Crystal chandeliers hang from the ceiling. The girls loved to go in there and twirl around like ballerinas. Also on the first floor was the huge formal dining room. A large door led into the kitchen. The kitchen was large but inviting. It was where the family ate most of their meals. There was a fireplace and a small sitting area there. At one end there was a large window that overlooked the back porch. This is where Emily sat at a table there to do her Bible study and prayer time. On the porch was a large sitting area that had chairs and a swing. Here is the place she loved to watch the morning sun rise.

The second floor was what the girls called the home floor. On this floor were the bedroom suites. Hers and Alex's room was a large room and bathroom. In her room there was a sitting area by a fireplace. The girl's rooms included bathrooms and sitting areas as well. Ariel's room which she picked out herself, had a large window seat overlooking the back of the manor. There were also four other smaller bedrooms with bathrooms on this floor. A large room at one end that was well lit had a small bathroom and every kind of toy imaginable in it. It was the girl's toy room. Nancy called it the dream playroom.

The third floor was clean and inviting. It consisted of twelve bedrooms with attached bathrooms. Each bedroom was furnished and comfortable. There was a stairway that led to and upper landing. Alex went up the stairs to the landing and found a doorway he told Emily to come up. They climbed a few stairs and opened a door to an attic. Emily stepped inside but suddenly it was like a hand was holding her back. She turned to Alex, "Let's not go here yet. I don't think the time is right." He wasn't sure why she said that but he had learned to trust her instincts.

Together they went back down to find the girls who were in the play room. Emily shook off the feeling she had from being in the attic. Alex sat on the floor and began playing with the girls. Emily watched them for a while feeling blessed. Alex looked up at her while she sat in a chair. "Wanna' play?" He now was in a playful happy mood. He stood up and crossed over to a window. Looking out he saw someone drive up to the barn. He turned and said "I haven't seen that truck before." Emily looked out as a man and a woman got out of the truck. She looked at Alex and together they went down to meet the visitors. Outside the day was slightly cool and as they crossed the yard to the barn, Larry and Carl came out and greeted the couple. Alex and Emily walked up and Larry introduced them, "Alex and Emily Daniels this is Dr. Bob Gordon and his wife Sara. He runs the small hospital and clinic in town. Dr. Bob this is Emily, Mr. Jarrod's niece."

Dr. Gordon shook hands with Alex and told him, "We used to come on a regular basis. Jarrod was my friend and patient. It is certainly an honor to meet you."

Emily invited them in for coffee. While enjoying their company, Emily found that the doctor often made house calls which rarely happened back home. The visit really made Emily miss not having a network of friends. Her days spent with her family had been enjoyable, but she needed outside friends as well. Growing up as a preacher's daughter gave her constant interaction with others. Now she missed it more than she ever thought she would.

After the doctor and his wife left she had turned to Alex, "I am so glad they came. It is nice to meet new people." Alex knew in his heart that his wife was still not happy here. He wondered how he could change that for her. He put his arm around her and answered, "Yes it was good to meet them. Honey I have been thinking about that front parlor where you are doing your sewing. I think I could turn it into a great sewing room where you can work and design your outfits."

Emily's eyes lit up with joy. Together they went to examine the room. Alex went out to the barn and came back with Carl and Larry at his side. They began measuring and talking as Emily sat down with a pad and pencil began drawing. She laid out the room design and showed it to the men. For the next few weeks furniture was moved and shelves were built. Alex and Larry made two large tables and a desk. When all was done she had a room she had always dreamed about having. Emily saw the room, but Alex saw the twinkle in her eyes that he had missed.

Months passed and soon Christmas rolled around and although it was summer in Australia the family loved the season. They called home, but her parents were unable to make the trip at this time. Even without family there, they enjoyed a very wonderful Christmas. Emily loved being able to give gifts. She made gifts for the staff and also gave them bonuses. The heartfelt thanks they expressed made Emily glad that all of them were in her life.

Emily kept busy in the following months making quilts and sweaters for the coming winter months. She loved writing in her journal and spent time studying God's Word. Seeking to stay as busy as possible she found projects to occupy her time. Even though she loved writing and quiet time with God, she could not get the uneasy feelings to subside. If only it would go away she thought after making her daily journal entry. Talking to God was always helpful, but she needed a friend outside the family with whom she could talk.

Everyone had settled in and considered this home. Emily was beginning to feel more at home here, but she longed for parts of her old life. Maybe if she just got out and did something it would cheer her up.

If she didn't get out she would put a damper on everything and soon her gloom would be responsible for bringing everyone else down. She started taking long walks along the driveway and once she ventured down the road about a half mile from the manor. She turned around at a huge ditch. Momentarily she paused to look around. There was something familiar about it but she shrugged her shoulders and walked back to the manor. Kate told her that soon the bad weather would begin and it would be harder to go into town. Emily decided tomorrow would be the day to get out and about. She realized that she had to let her life in the states go and accept that this was now her home. Everyone else loved it here and she was determined that she would also.

Alex had spent time with her teaching her to drive on the left side of the road and helping her to become acquainted with driving rules and regulations in Australia. Finally she felt comfortable driving, but she had never ventured out on her own. The next morning she set out in the car with anticipation. After designing some new dresses, she was anxious to find material to make them. She also had decided to find material to make Alex some new shirts. The girls also need new pants and dresses. Alex's redesigned parlor-sewing room was a place where she could design and create. Since the creation of this room she now spent a great deal of her time there. She felt right about this trip to town, and something inside her was telling her the time was right. As she drove along she found it peaceful to be alone in the car. She spent time praying and talking to God. It was a bit of an alone time within itself. Asking herself questions she soon wondered, "What will I find there? What if I don't like it at all? Then a wave of panic hit her, What am I doing? Just as quickly as the insecurities came she had a word from God. 'I will never leave thee or forsake thee.' Emily prayed and asked God for His guidance in this trip. Knowing that the fear and uncertainty came from Satan, she dismissed them. Little did she know that a simple shopping trip would be a turning point in her life. In fact, it brought many changes to everyone. It came to mean the first step to God's perfect plan for her.

CHAPTER
FOUR

~

The town was small but very convenient to where they lived. Only a few small shops adorned the street. Somehow the whole atmosphere of quiet and peacefulness surrounding the town gave Emily a sense of calm as she pulled into the parking space in front of the fabric shop.

As Emily stepped out of her car she looked up and down the street to take in all the feeling of the charm of the area. Emily was always active and outgoing at home and it was hard to believe that it had been seven months since she left the ranch. The general settling in to her surroundings had taken most of her time. She redecorated the girls rooms and then Alex had spent time setting up her sewing room. She now had to supply her new room. She looked at this day as exciting and could not wait to shop and explore her new town.

As she entered the fabric shop she was extremely surprised at the grand selection of fabrics and sewing supplies that the small store offered. Not expecting her task to be so hard, she decided to stock up on several types of fabrics and supplies. After all now she had plenty of room to stock up. Some of the fabrics would be new clothes for her family-dresses, shirts, pants, lingerie, and some would be for decorating, quilts, pillows, and curtains. In addition to fabrics she bought zippers, buttons, thread, batting as well as yarn for knitting and crochet items. She had begun teaching the girls to knit and crochet and also sewing small items. As she fingered the baby cord she remembered Alex's words that morning, "Em, you amaze me! With all the money we have you could buy clothes and other things. Why do you want to spend all this time sewing?" He had smiled and kissed her and patted her cheek as he turned to leave for his work on the ranch. She added, "And why do you have to work?" He realized that just as he liked working she too liked sewing. She smiled as she examined the fabrics and realized how excited she really was to get to designing and sewing again. Every year for Christmas she had made quilts, blankets and gifts for her family and friends. Because of the move, she had sent money the first year. But this year she would send gifts and money.

The shop owner helped load everything in her SUV. She thanked the owner and as she turned to go to her SUV, she ran into a man and woman. She dropped some of the packages she was still carrying. Bending over to retrieve her things, she began to apologize. "I am sorry." The man helped her to pick up the packages and even helped get them into the car. "Thank you so much."

"Hello, it's nice to meet you or run into you," he grinned and offered his hand.

"Oh thank you and I am so sorry. I wasn't watching where I was going. I am Emily Daniels."

"Hi I am Mark Garrett and this is my wife, Robyn."

Robyn smiled and shook Emily's hand, "It is so good to meet you. We don't see many new people here. Our town is not a tourist location."

Mark was pretending to dust dirt from his jacket, and jokingly acted like he was annoyed. Robyn pushed him a little and laughed, "This clown loves to joke around. You just never know when he is serious!"

"Clown am I, now," He laughed and poked Robyn playfully. "We were going for lunch. Would you like to join us?"

"Thank you, I wasn't looking forward to eating alone. I had thought about finishing my shopping and then going on home."

"You can't drive on an empty stomach." Mark still grinning impishly.

They went to a restaurant close by and after they ordered, Mark began asking her a battery of questions. "What is an American doing here? Are you visiting relatives close by?"

Robyn stopped him, "My goodness aren't you being a bit nosey today?"

"That is fine, I don't mind. It's been seven months since moving here and it is good to meet new people." She looked at Mark and grinned, "Even nosy ones, the only people I have talked with are my family, the staff and workers at the ranch. My uncle Jarrod McLeod left his ranch to me, with the stipulation that I move here and live on the property. I was getting tired of not having much to do, so I ventured into town to buy sewing supplies."

"Oh this is so exciting!" Robyn exclaimed. "We are neighbors. I hope we didn't make a bad first impression." She jabbed Mark in his side. He playfully acted hurt.

"I am so glad! I am not used to not having neighbors and even though I have a wonderful place to live I miss people."

"We have visited many times with your uncle and we liked him very much. It was sad to see him die." Mark added. "We have been out of the country on business. It usually keeps us traveling for months at a time. We needed to stock up on supplies and came to town. We would have come by to welcome you sooner had we been here."

"I am so glad you are home now. I look forward to having neighbors."

"Do you have children, Emily?" Robyn asked.

"Yes I have three daughters. Do you have children?"

"We have five children." Mark said, "You know long cold Australian winters and all."

"Will you stop?" Robyn jabbed him.

To which he mischievously added, "I will if you will."

They all laughed. "Seriously we have four boys and one girl." Robyn continued.

"The girls will be so glad to have neighbors as well."

Emily found her time with the Garretts very relaxing. Soon they were talking like old friends and joking around with each other. Mark teased her about being a reckless walker and wanted to know if she drove the same way. Mark looked at his watch and commented, "Well ladies I have to take the food supplies home and pick up some feed for the animals. Also the kids will be home soon."

"Mark I haven't finished shopping."

"I could take you home." Emily offered.

Turning to leave he teased, "Be careful on the sidewalks." Robyn just shook her head and Mark smiled. Then stopped, "Are you sure you are a safe driver? That's my special cargo there." He leaned down and kissed Robyn and waved bye to Emily.

"He loves to act silly, but he is a good man." Robyn stared after him as he left.

Robyn took her to an art supply store so she could get art supplies for her design projects and also for the girl's art projects-especially, for Nancy because she seemed to use them the most. She discovered that Robyn and Mark had five children, Hank, twins-Edward and Erika, Wesley and Lois. Hank was Leigha's age, Edward and Erika were Nancy's age and Wesley was Ariel's age and Louis just a year younger than Ariel. Emily had a great time with Robyn and was very excited to get home and share the outing with the family. She found her way to the Garrett's place easily. It was a large house as well. It was two stories in the middle, but most of it was sprawled out. It was a pretty light salmon colored brick. Emily hated for her day to end.

"Robyn, would you, Mark and your children like to come for dinner tomorrow?"

"That would be wonderful! It would be fun to have our families get together."

"Well how does six sound? Come earlier so we can visit,"

"Maybe someday you can teach me to sew."

As she was leaving Mark and the children drove up. He stopped and stuck his head out, "I see you got her home safe." He let out a big laugh. She shook her head and smiled as she waved bye.

As Emily drove home she kept thinking how blessed she was to have new friends.

Now she understood why God had put this trip in her mind. He always knows just what I need when I need it. She smiled and starting singing, *"In the morning sunlight, He is there. In the shades of midnight, He is there. There's no need to worry; there's no need to care; 'cause everywhere I go I know that God is there."* She could have gone any day, but today she met new friends. "Thank you Lord!" As she drove home she felt very calm and happy.

Emily knew that God had met her needs. Her thoughts flowed over her mind. I hope that Kate doesn't mind the extra work. Oh please let Alex like them and also the kids get along. It will be so nice to have close friends again. I hope we can all be close. Looking up ahead she saw home and realized finally she thought of this place as home. She pulled up to the back of the house and the ladies came out with her girls close behind to begin unloading the packages. "Hey Mom did you leave anything in town?" Leigha laughed. Larry was also helping them unload and laughed, "I guess you are making up for lost shopping days."

Once inside Emily excitedly told them about her day, "Oh Kate I hope you don't mind, but I invited the Garret family to dinner tomorrow."

Kate was so glad to see the change in Emily, "Of course that will be fine. I have steaks planned or do you prefer something else."

"That will be fine and I will help anyway that you want me to help."

"No need Ms. Emily, the ladies and I receive a paycheck for doing this!" she laughed.

Emily smiled and gave Kate a hug. Emily and her girls went to put her packages away.

Larry hugged his wife, "Maybe she should have gone shopping sooner. She is definitely in a good mood. Did you notice how pretty she looked with that smile on her face? It just lit up the room."

"Get to work mister." she laughed. "This is just what she needs."

Emily came back to the kitchen and explained, "Oh yes, Kate the Garretts have five children."

"We have cooked for over 220 people before. Don't worry."

"I am sorry Kate. I have never had employees before. Besides you are more like family than employee." Emily laughed.

Larry asked, "Is that Mr. Mark Garret?"

"Yes do you know them? They were so easy to get to know. I felt like I had known them for years."

"As a matter of fact, I have known Mr. Mark since he was a baby. I helped out on his place when I was younger. My father was foreman on his station and now my brother is."

Emily smiled and couldn't believe what a small world this had become. She asked,

"Oh by the way, Larry do you know where Alex is working today?" Not really giving him time to answer her question, she continued, "Do you think they will like us?"

Larry laughed and said "I will go get Alex because I know he will want to hear the news you have." He left with a smile on his face.

Kate answered Emily's last question, "I don't see any reason they wouldn't like you! They are good Christian people, so I think that alone gives you a lot in common. They are gone much of the time, but my sister-in-law is their housekeeper and she says this was to be their last trip for a while."

"What does he do for a living? He said he was gone on business."

"He is in the entertainment business. He is a movie director, but he has been very unhappy with his work lately. He doesn't like the trend that movies are taking today."

"Oh I really hope they stay awhile. Maybe he just needs a break to be able to see what needs to be done." Emily smiled, "Kate I feel like a new person; I really needed this day. I feel that God has so blessed me."

"Yes He has and now I can see the real Emily standing in front of me." Kate patted Emily's shoulder. "I believe I see Alex and the girls in the corral. They've been riding. You should go tell them the news."

Emily left the kitchen and ran out to the barn shouting, "Alex! Girls! I have great news!"

They ran out to meet her, excited to see her in such a happy mood. Seeing her so happy made them wonder what had made the change in her. Alex saw his Emily all bright and smiling with all her beauty shining out from her face. He realized just how much he loved her. "Hey sweetheart! What is the happy news? You look so cheerful."

"Oh I am!" she smiled up at Alex as he reached out to her hug. "I met our neighbors the Garretts and they are great. They have five children and I invited them for dinner tomorrow." She spoke in short sentences in her enthusiasm to include all the information.

"Okay now just calm down a bit before you swallow your tongue." He laughed.

"Oh Alex, God answered my prayers. He meant for me to be there. I literally bumped into them on the sidewalk. Their kids are all around the same ages as our girls. They have four boys and a girl. Isn't it amazing?"

The girls starting laughing and talking at the same time! "Did you say boys?" Leigha asked. "How old are they and are they cute?"

Emily laughed at that question and stopped for a moment to realize her daughter was growing up. "Well now you would find that interesting?" Grinning at her daughter, she explained, "Well Hank is the oldest and I think he is your age, Edward and Erika are twins and I think they are Nancy's age, Wesley is Ariel's age and Louis is a year younger than her, as far as the cute part their parents are very nice looking so more than likely they will be, too. We will just have to wait and see. They are going to be here tomorrow for dinner." Emily smiled at her girls and realized they were as excited about new friends as she was.

"What will we wear?" Ariel inquired.

"I finished those new outfits last night and they are all ready for you."

"Of course you did!" Nancy laughed.

They all arm in arm went to the house. Everyone was talking happily.

Alex with his arm around his beautiful wife said, "Well honey, I think this is just what you needed!"

After they were finished with supper, they had their Bible study and devotional for the evening. The girls had all thanked God for new friends and for making their Mom happy again.

The girls went to get ready for bed and Emily and Alex followed them upstairs to tuck the girls in and say good-night. While waiting Alex pulled Emily close and tenderly smiled down at her. "It is so good to see you like this. I have missed you!" He kissed her, and continued, "I was worried about you. You are always hiding your feelings so as not to worry others. I didn't know how to get through to you. Now I see my Emily."

"Oh Babe I am so sorry. I guess I didn't realize how much I missed my friends back in Arkansas."

"You know that is the first time you haven't said 'Back home'."

"I finally feel like this is home. Wait until you meet them. Robyn, Mrs. Garrett, is so nice and easy to get to know. Talking with her was like conversing with an old friend. Mark is extremely pleasant even for a big movie director, but of course I have never met a director before, nevertheless he is very welcoming. I think you will like him." Emily was talking very fast and excitedly.

"Oh you think so?" Alex's eyes twinkled as he listened to her. Seeing her so happy he thought, *"She's back."*

"Yeah I do. He is witty just like you." She playfully jabbed him in the ribs and then ran away. He scooped her up and swung her up on his shoulder laughing. This brought a round of giggles and applause from the girls.

Leigha standing in the hallway exclaimed, "Dad! Mom! I don't think you two will ever grow up!"

Alex laughingly put Emily down and Emily smiled and said, "Now that I have my dignity back," Cutting her eyes over at Alex playfully, "I see you girls are ready for bed so scoot and go to bed." After prayers they tucked the children in and kissed them good-night, Alex and Emily went to their room.

"I think the girls are excited to meet new friends."

"You know, Em, God always knows what we need." Alex smiled and began to get ready for bed.

"It always seems that God leads me to the important things in my life. God was in this day, after all I never even wanted to go in to town before, but He laid it on my heart to go today. Then the first thing I meet new friends."

"Kind of like the day we met?" He grinned. "Now tell me exactly how you met them? Ran them over on the sidewalk? Wouldn't it have been easier to just introduce yourself?" He chuckled pulling her into his arms and smiled lovingly at his pretty wife. His bright blue eyes held a hint of mischief in them.

Emily looked up into his face and grinned. "Well you do what you have to do!"

Alex took her in his arms and tenderly kissed her. "You have been so lonesome and I didn't know how to help you. You are always hiding your feelings when you have an inner conflict." He drew her closer and then continued, "It makes it hard at times to talk to you when you keep saying that everything is okay. I know that it isn't because I can still see the worry in your eyes."

"I know and I don't know why I do that, except I don't want you to worry about me. It takes me time to process some feelings. Maybe I need to be more patient and rely on God more than I do."

"Processing is what you also gave to your youngest. Ariel does that too. I have a feeling she learned it from you. I do wish that you would open up more; I do love you, you know," Alex and Emily walked to the bed and he continued as they got into the bed. "This place and this whole path has been such a blessing to me and I wanted you to love it too."

"I think I am seeing things in a different light, and it just took me longer to let go of Arkansas."

"You have always been a little slow on the uptake." Alex said in a mock accent. "Well I think we need to engage in a little extracurricular activity." Alex raised his eyebrows flirtingly, "Wanna' build a tricycle motor? I promise, It'll be fun!" Emily grinned and snuggled into his arms and he added with tender devotion, "You are the best thing that has ever happened to me."

The next evening the Garrets arrived at 6:00; immediately the children seemed to connect with each other. They were laughing and talking like old friends almost instantaneously. During dinner they chatted away. Mark and Alex seemed relaxed with each other as well. After dinner the children ran out to the corral to see the horses. Leigha and Hank seemed to be at very comfortable with each other's company.

Mark watching them said, "I don't think I have ever seen Hank talkative around a girl before. Usually he doesn't have much to say at all."

Robyn added, "He is usually very shy with new people, and very rarely warms up to girls, and just look at them. It's amazing."

"Leigha has a way with people. They just seem to feel at ease around her. It's the same effect that her Mom had on me." Alex winked at Emily.

"You are full of it! He is the one who got me to talk. At first I wouldn't talk at all. Of course, we have been in love since I was only twelve."

"Yes I had to wait for her to grow up," Alex explained. "We were neighbors and even though she was young I noticed her early on. I never knew she would grow up to be such a fine lady. But I have had a hard time 'raising' her…she can be very stubborn. As you have seen first- hand, she can be quite a bit if a klutz. We move to a new place and she goes around running over people who are trying to walk down the sidewalk." Alex rolled his eyes playfully and everyone was laughing.

"He loves picking on me." Emily blushing poked him in the side with her elbow.

Robyn queried, "Did you really love him when you were twelve?"

"Yes, I had a crush to end all crushes. Of course he never even knew I existed. He was a bit older than I was, and I think every girl in town was after him. I used to have dreams that I was grown and he asked me out. I was so short and plain compared to the girls that came around him!" Emily sighed and then said, "I had a pretend diary where I would pretend that we were boyfriend and girlfriend. It was how I coped with not being old enough to tell him how I felt."

Mark leaned over and apparently interested in the story, asked Alex, "I am a bit curious, did you know that she loved you? When did you fall in love with her?"

"Mark! You are so nosy and I know that you always like a good love story." Robyn added shaking her head. "Just be careful Alex he will want to make a movie out of it."

Alex lifted his hand, "It's okay. I love the story myself. It is really kind of mystical in a way. Strangely enough, the age difference never really seemed to come into the picture. The first time I noticed her she was about 10. I told my Dad that I had been born too soon. She was tiny and fragile and very cute. At first I thought she was a sweet little girl. Watching her grow up wasn't easy. Often I tried to just act like a big brother type; once I took her and my niece to the fair for my sister-in-law.

It seemed like the more I was around her the more she permeated my thoughts. I would imagine her grown up and then I would feel ashamed like I shouldn't be thinking of her like that. Then, I joined the Navy and four years later, when I returned she was 16 and I had fallen hopelessly in love with her. She wrote the sweetest most innocent letters to me while I was on board the aircraft carrier where I served. I can't explain it but I always felt like we belonged together. It was really tough at times, but I was an older man and I never knew how to approach her without seeming like I was a pervert. I would often wonder if she ever thought about dating an older guy or if she ever thought about me at all. While I was in the Navy her letters were mainly about what was happening in the states. She had asked me if I was saved in one of them. It was so heart felt when she told me how glad that she was that I knew the Lord. After I came home, I went to all her high school ballgames and then she started dating this guy named Curtis. He came around every day and I found myself resenting him being close to her. Several times I watched them on her front porch as he tried to kiss her and she would push him away; I wanted to go over there and punch him. I knew I was in danger of letting my feelings cause me to lose my sanity. My Dad would talk to me about it and without his guidance I feel like I might have made a mess of it." Alex paused and then continued his story. "His advice was to leave it alone and leave it up to God. He told me, "If it is meant to be it will be. If God's hand is in it nothing will keep you apart." I was so obsessed that it was hard to sit back and not do anything. I ignored my instincts to jump right in and solve it all, but I listened to my Father's advice. After praying with my Father I waited on God and His hand was in it. I know that now beyond a shadow of a doubt." He smiled tenderly at Emily who was very surprised and knew that Alex was comfortable with these new friends. She had never seen him get so serious and rarely ever shared his personal feelings.

Mark was excited, "This is a great love story…wow what a story. Tell me more; I could listen to this all day."

Robyn chimed in, "Now I feel nosy, but I want to hear more too."

Alex stretched out his long muscular legs and continued his story, "We would see each other at Brian's my brother's house every now and then. Emily was still dating Curtis and I was worried that I might not ever get a chance to tell her how I felt or even if she would ever date me. One day I went over to her house and found her in the front yard crying. It was just after Curtis had stormed off of her porch. My heart stood still, and I wanted to take her in my arms to comfort her. I wanted to tell her I would never let anyone hurt her again. So, I went over and asked her if I could help her. She was so shy, and said that she didn't want to bother anyone with her problem. By the way that is something she still does!" He shot Emily a knowing look. Emily shook her head and smiled. "Well, I took her face in my hands and wiped away her tears. I told her I would help if I could. At that moment all I wanted was for her problem to be mine so she wouldn't hurt any more. I think at that moment my heart was hers even if we never got together."

Emily looked surprised, "I thought you were just being nice. Curtis had just told me that he wanted someone he could be with...you know in the way a married couple were, but without the marriage part." She blushed in her description.

"I am glad I never knew that then. Let's say that battle is one the devil would have won if you know what I mean." Alex stated firmly.

"When did you first think he had noticed you, Emily?" Mark asked

"Well I went to his niece's house and he was in the kitchen talking to his sister. When we entered the kitchen, he jumped up and knocked over his glass and his chair. I wanted to laugh but I was afraid it would embarrass him if I did."

"If you had only known, I had just asked my sister-in-law if she thought it was okay if I dated someone that many years younger than me. Then she walks in with this cute white sun dress on and a pretty green ribbon in her long black hair. She looked like an angel. I had come to the point that I didn't trust myself to be in the same room with her. Mainly, I was afraid of showing how I felt and scaring her away. One thing that always worried me was the small town where we lived; there were so many gossipy tongues there. I didn't want to do anything that would cause anyone to think less of Emily. I didn't care one bit what they thought of me."

"So when did you end up together?" Mark asked as Robyn nodded in agreement that she wanted to know too.

"My sister who was there and my niece, Donna convinced me to ask her out. She gave me this sad story that Emily and the guy she was dating had broken up and Emily didn't have a date for the prom. She said if I asked her out then maybe Emily would ask me to take her to the prom and wouldn't have to go alone. Needless to say Donna also used the fact that Curtis was going alone from what she had heard." He looked at Emily and continued his story, "At that moment I didn't care how old I was, and if it meant going to the prom well needless to say nobody had to twist my arm. Somehow I had a feeling that this was my chance. Actually my niece had overheard me asking my sister-in-law about dating a younger woman and after she saw my reaction when Emily entered, she put two and two together. Donna also knew that Emily was in love with someone but didn't think it would ever be possible to have a chance to date him. Donna noticed the expression on Emily's face that day, too. I think that is when Donna figured that I was Emily's love. Later she told Emily that her uncle wanted to date her, but was afraid to ask her out." He stopped and looked at his beautiful wife.

"The first date was awesome and I think I was walking the streets of gold. One date led to another and yes we went to the prom." Emily laughed and smiled at Alex.

"After just six weeks of dating, I could not wait any longer, so I asked her to marry me. 'I was so happy I cried!" Emily added.

"I wasn't taking any chances of losing her. I wasn't getting any younger and I really felt God was answering my prayers. No one could ever convince me otherwise. Things just fell into place. I went to her dad and asked for her hand, and he and I both joked with her later that her dad laughed and told me he didn't think he would ever get rid of her."

"We are very blessed with a God given relationship." Emily spoke up, "As long as we keep God in our marriage He will bless us."

Alex was beginning to become uneasy with the seriousness of this story. Aware that he was sharing his personal feelings, he asked Mark, "Enough about us. How did you two meet?"

"Ours is not quite so romantic; we met at the hospital where we both worked."

"Mark and I were working at the same hospital and just started dating. It wasn't romantic but it was hilarious. Mark was an orderly and he had to pick up and deliver patients... and sometimes deceased patients. One day he pretended to be a dead body. One of his friends parked the gurney he was on in front of the nurse's station where I worked as a ward secretary. It was covered with a sheet and he had a toe tag on his foot just like a dead body on its way to the morgue would have. His buddy asked me to keep an eye on the body while he went to the restroom. All of a sudden Mark sat straight up. Of course I screamed." Robyn laughed.

"She got me fired!" Mark acting wounded continued the story. "Everyone on the whole floor came running to see what was happening."

"Mark has always been a bit of a comedian without much of a filter. But I guess that's one of the reasons I love him! He makes me laugh."

Gradually their conversations switched to ranch life and Alex and Mark went off to the barn to check on the kids.

"I would love to see some of your designs that you told me about, if that's okay?" Robyn asked. Do you have any finished outfits to show?

"That's easy-this outfit I have on, Alex's shirt and the girls outfits are all my designs.

"You are good."

Emily took Robyn to see her sewing room. "This room is awesome." Robyn commented as she looked around the room. The room had once been a formal sitting room, but Alex had changed it to be her sewing room. One side of the room held shelves of neatly folded fabrics. There were bins of colored yarns on the bottom shelves. One corner included a large cutting table, and several sewing forms in that area. Toward the center there was a large work area. Three types of sewing machines were on the shelves under the work table, and an area for sewing was in front of a window. A drawing table sat in front of another window. Both windows were large and received natural light. This is where Emily sat to draw her designs. Looking up Robyn saw a huge quilting frame that hung from the ceiling. It had a brightly colored quilt on it.

"This room is a dream. If I had a room like this I would never leave."

"I do spend a great deal of my time here, when I am not teaching the girls their lessons. Alex and I designed the room together."

. "I have three new designs on which I am working now" Emily showed her designs to Robyn.

"These designs are very good, Emily. Do you design all your own clothes?" Robyn carefully looked at Emily's designs. "Do you ever sell any of your designs?"

"No not sell. I have sewn for friends and family."

"Do you mind if I show these to Mark?"

"Of course you can, but why would he be interested in my work?"

"Well his next movie is here in Australia, and he was worried about the designs, because no one could quite give him what he wanted. Maybe you can listen to what he wants and help him out."

"You really think I am that good?"

Robyn nodded her head, as they heard Alex and Mark in the hallway deciding to help each other unload feed tomorrow. The kids had just gone upstairs in the game room as the guys were entering the sewing room, "This is what I helped Emily design for her work room." Alex was explaining to Mark as they entered.

"This is a very nice room. Now, Robyn is going to want one too." He joked and winked at Robyn. She made a face at him, "I will hold you to that Mr. Smarty Pants."

"Come look at these." Robyn motioned for Mark to look at Emily's designs. "Emily is going to teach me to sew so that may be a good idea you had, but this is what I want you to see."

Mark took the sketches and carefully examined each one. He looked at Emily as if he was seeing her for the first time. He had no problem seeing and understanding Alex's devotion to her. She did have a very feminine quality about her that caused a man to want to protect her. "I like these. You have a real talent. Do you think you could design something futuristic? That is without being cliché" Mark was very interested in her work.

"I could try." Emily shyly answered.

"We are doing a movie about life after the big bomb. Some survivors are living in a future type world. Everything I have seen. . . Well they are just not right. I need something new."

Alex looked at Emily and said, "Wait just a minute."

Mark felt the bound between Alex and Emily, and wondered *'Is this what being 'one' is? It's like they could read each other's mind.'*

Alex walked over to a file cabinet and took out a folder. As he handed it to Mark he winked at Emily and said, "I read your mind for a change." Looking at Mark's expressions as he examined the folder he knew that Emily had done it again.

"These are incredible! I can't believe it!" As Mark looked from Emily to Alex he motioned for Robyn to come and look at the designs. "It's like she crawled inside my head and took pictures of what I wanted." He was ecstatic. "This is just what I have been looking for." He crossed over to Emily and picked her up and swung her around. "OOPs I am sorry." Looking embarrassed as he put her down.

"Mark gets carried away sometimes." Robyn apologized.

"It looks like the incredible Emily Daniels has done it again!" Alex commented, "I guess there is something you need to know about my Emily now. She reads minds, sees the future, and has an intuition that will knock your socks off!" Alex explained, "She drew these the day before she drove into town and met you."

Alex meant it as a joke and everyone laughed. Still it made Emily feel very self-conscious. More times than she could remember what Alex called her intuition had led her to know things. As she looked at everyone in the room her strange feeling returned. Somehow she felt that those feelings had to do with the people in this room. She wasn't sure if it was good or bad. Emily looked at Robyn and felt a shiver run down her spine and a sudden feeling of loss. She had been standing back and listening to everyone laugh and talk. Alex sensing her extreme quietness walked over and put his arm around her shoulders.

"I have a business trip in three days. May I borrow these?" Mark asked then continued, "On second thought, why don't you two go with us?

Robyn spoke up, "That would be so much fun! My mother is keeping my kids. Would Kate and Larry watch yours?"

"It sounds like fun Emily. What do you say?" Alex inquired.

"Sure why not?" Emily smiled. "I feel like we have known you both forever."

The rest of the evening was taken up in planning the trip. It turned out to be the first of many trips and it was interesting how their lives became intertwined from the very beginning.

CHAPTER
FIVE

~

The trip to Sydney was even more eventful than it had been the first time they were here. Robyn and Emily spent hours shopping while Alex and Mark went to Mark's meetings. At lunch they met at a restaurant that was one of Mark's favorite places. After lunch they all went on a sight-seeing expedition. Mark and Robyn showed them some places they hadn't seen before with Richard and Catherine, who joined them for dinner that evening. Richard set up appointments with them to visit and become acquainted with the McLeod advertising business. Alex's MBA would come in handy while learning the business. Emily decided that Alex should be the one to handle this aspect of her inheritance. Explaining to Richard that Alex had the knack for business and her talents were elsewhere. Mark told her that his production company had accepted her designs and had papers drawn up for her sell them. Emily decided to take the money from the sell of the designs and invest in Mark's company.

Catherine loved Emily's designs and asked her to design a gown for her. Emily agreed and set up a time for her to come for a fitting. Little did Emily know that this day was the beginning for her in the design business.

Alex discovered that he was at ease with his duties and position in the business world. He took to it almost as quickly as he did to the ranch life. Mark had put Emily in charge of the design part of his business. She had laughed when he asked her how it felt to be a boss. It was exciting to meet actors and actresses that came for fittings. Everything was in a whirlwind trying to achieve as much as possible in a short time. Emily found herself enjoying her life as well. It was obvious that things were falling in place, but she missed the security of the ranch. She still had found time for her morning quiet time with God and her Bible study, although she missed the beautiful sunrises from her porch at home. Yes, home, she thought. Australia was now home to her and she felt a bit of peace at the thought.

Robyn came by and they went to breakfast.

"Robyn, how do you get use to this fast lifestyle?"

"That's why Mark and I have decided to make things simpler for ourselves. You never really get used to it. Either you like it or you don't. Sometimes the biggest part is just trying to fit in. I don't think we really ever have!"

"Why do you stay with it? Is it financial?"

"No not really, maybe at first it was. Now we have enough set aside to taper our involvement for a while. This is going to be Mark's last picture for a while. It was already in the making when we decided it was time to slow down. He is close to burnout but it may be hard to come back after staying out of the business for a time. However that is a chance we are willing to take. We have the production company and our place is paid off. We just need time to relax and spend time with our family. The children are growing up so fast. I realized that more as I watched Hank and Leigha."

"I understand that! You know with Mark's good looks he would have been an excellent leading man; well that is if he likes acting."

"He liked acting and was really quite good at it, but the scripts that he was offered disgusted him. It seems like all they had was sex films and filled with unnecessary foul language that added absolutely nothing to the plot. He would come home at night and be in such foul moods because even having to repeat the words that made him sick. He was so repulsed by it that he decided to go into directing and producing, so he could choose his own scripts."

"I see how that could sicken anyone. They just don't have decent writers anymore." Emily commented.

"Too bad we aren't writers, we could write a romance about real love, not just sex." Robyn grinned.

"Sometimes it is better to leave a little bit to the imagination!" Emily chuckled.

They laughed at the thought and continued with breakfast.

As they finished and were leaving Robyn said, "You know Mark is thinking about going into producing and directing Christian films only. He has had some bad times even in directing.

Dealing with everything became just as distasteful as acting. He said that in directing he had to deal with every scene not just ones he was in."

"You know it seems like they not only exploit women, but men also nowadays." Emily added.

"Interesting that you would say that, Mark never liked acting because he said he often felt like a piece of meat on a plate. His directing has had its problems as well. The last two pictures were extremely rough. The actresses were very picky." Robyn rolled her eyes.

"That's what I have heard and some of them have no morals." Emily shook her head.

"You are right! Some of them will do anything to get a part. One of the starlets broke into our hotel room and got in the bathtub. She didn't know I was there and so I found her and oh the lies she told. I told her to get out and she better be glad that I found her and not Hank. She said that she had no idea that he traveled with his wife and kids. No remorse on her part whatsoever! It was like I was at fault for being there with my husband." Robyn said disgustingly.

"Oh no, I can't imagine!" Emily sympathized.

"I can see why so many of the marriages don't work out. I don't want anything to ever happen to Mark and I. We have always communicated and of course our faith in God also helps!"

"Has Mark ever given you any reasons to doubt him?"

"No, and I hope to keep it that way. Sometimes I am ashamed of myself when I get jealous. Mark is so good to me and always faithful trying to never get into any situations that could cause me pain. Do you mind if I ask you how you and Alex got so close? I thought Mark and I have always been close, but you two are in a separate league!"

"I don't think you have to worry. Mark's eyes shine when he looks at you. And as far as Alex and me…the only thing I can say is that our love for each other and our faith in God has made us close. We have had to work at it. At first Alex was very insecure because of our age difference, and I too was not sure that I deserved him. I think our first few years were spent in just getting sure of ourselves. Alex and I both were raised in Christian homes and we pray and study God's Word always trying to seek His guidance. Sometimes each argument or hardship just seemed to bring us closer. I guess we over communicated to the point that we seemed to know what each other's thoughts were. It can also be a curse as well as a blessing. A lot of times it has been a headache!" Emily laughed.

"I don't see how! You two just gush love!"

"Oh give me a break! You should be a writer, talk about dramatic!" Emily laughed partially because of the statement and also because she was a bit embarrassed by the complement. "The love is always good, but the closeness has its down side. You start sensing things…" She wondered if she could share her strange feelings about Alex. Deciding to keep them to herself she continued, "That can cause you to worry sometimes."

"How do you mean?" Robyn sensed that there was more to Emily than she was sharing.

"I don't talk about this often, but it's my intuition that Alex always jokes about." She gulped and then continued, "Short of having friends thinking I am crazy, mostly I just keep it to myself. Sometimes I just seem to know things. I don't know why and it scares me a little, especially when I am right. I think the Lord gave it to me, but I don't always understand it. Alex jokes about it but I know at times he is uneasy about it too." She looked away for a minute because the feeling that she had gotten when she first met Robyn flooded her mind. Really wanting to have someone to talk to about the strange feelings, she hesitated not wishing her new friend to think less of her. "Oh well, that's something we will talk more about later." She smiled at Robyn and said, "Are you sure you still want this crazy person for a friend?"

"Don't be silly! I think I need you as much as I think you need me. Let's have some fun and we will revisit this conversation later."

They took a water taxi around the bay and Emily took some pictures. They were laughing and talking when suddenly Emily had a strange feeling. She told Robyn that she wanted to get out and walk a little bit. As they got off of the taxi, Alex called out to her, "Em, over here."

"Wow! How did you know they were here?" Robyn looked at her with amazement. "I think you two are always in each other's thoughts!"

Emily just shrugged her shoulders as they walked toward Alex and Mark.

After business was completed they returned home for a few weeks. The pace of their lives increased over the next year. They made trips to location sites for the movie and often the kids accompanied them. The children were often used as part of the crowd on camera. It was a fun time but busy too. Alex noticed how she successfully handled the people with whom she worked. On many occasions he had overheard the actors or crew saying how easy working with her was. It made him feel proud. This was all exciting and different to them. Alex often felt that she was throwing herself so fully into this work that he wondered if she still had the unsettling feelings she had when they first arrived.

Robyn and Emily made several trips together and became close friends. The closer they became the more of herself Emily shared. One day she decided to tell Robyn about the dark feelings she had when they first arrived, "I have had an uneasy feeling since we came here. It unfortunately is a feeling of loss…a very dark feeling. It is a feeling that I am going to lose someone I care deeply about." She closed her eyes and tried to regain her composure.

"Are you sure it's not just the uncertainty of a new lifestyle and new surroundings?"

"Alex keeps telling me this. I prayed that God would help me know what it is or at least give me peace until He decides to reveal it to me."

"You share these feelings with Alex?" Robyn asked. "Does he understand?"

"Of course I do. We share everything even when it isn't pleasant. He is supportive."

Robyn sensed that Emily was becoming uncomfortable so she tried to lighten the mood. She said, "Well aren't we getting a bit morbid?"

Emily smiled and realized that she had stopped herself from telling Robyn about her feeling when they first met. They went to the set and Mark greeted them with a problem. Emily took it in stride and handled the situation like she had been doing this for years. Mark became increasingly amazed at her ability to adapt to changes almost instantly. He commented to Alex, "She makes me feel like she is inside my head just looking around to see what I want from this film. It seems like I just have to look at her and she knows what I want. Sometimes it scares me a little."

Alex laughed, "Now you know why I love her like I do. She knows how to make me love her by reading my mind." Even though the subject was familiar to him, he knew exactly how Mark felt. He too had often become a little unnerved by her premonitions.

"Alex you may joke about it but after these last few months, I believe she does have that ability! The takes have gone smoother and the cast and crew have gotten along better than ever. I have a very good feeling about this film."

"Emily told me that she felt good about it too." Alex explained, "It is better than the feelings she has been having about me."

"What's that?" Mark asked, sensing Alex's need to share.

"She said she feels like something bad will happen to me." Alex a very handsome man, looked a bit uncomfortable and tried to change the subject. "She is pretty great! At least I've always thought so."

Mark following his lead continued, "Well if she feels good about the film then so do I."

As they went about their business, Mark could clearly see that Alex and Emily were very close. He also realized that their closeness had also rubbed off on his and Robyn's marriage. They had a way of looking at life that just permeated those around them. They both could fit

Hollywood's vision of leading characters, but their attitudes and looks were from an inner beauty not a fake made up one. Alex had become more like a brother than just a friend. Because of their influence Mark and Robyn had grown closer to God. They attended the same church and had started Bible studies together. He and Robyn had accepted Christ as their Savior, but not until now had they really grown in faith. He finally felt that this film would do well and then he could spend time with his family. 'Perhaps that is why they all went into town that day.'

After the movie was finished Emily found herself just as busy. Some of the people involved in the movie business had asked her for gowns. These gowns were to be worn at the awards since Mark had received a nomination for best director and she had also been nominated for a design award. Her designs had achieved a great deal of attention. She made her and Robyn's dresses herself. Robyn had helped with the dresses getting better at sewing with each lesson Emily taught her. They would soon go to the states and Emily had even had an invitation to do an interview with a magazine. Although it was all very exciting Emily was ready for home and calmer days.

"Alex, I am ready for all this to be over so we can settle down to our old way of life again."

"Honey, I don't know that things will ever be the same again. Is all this wearing you down?"

"It is very tiring…although it is fun. I think the going here and there is the hardest part. I miss quiet times. I miss my sunrises on the porch at home."

"Yeah I do too." He drew her close and looked down at his fragile pretty wife. "It's been fun, but you are famous now and the entire world wants to see my beautiful wife."

"Alex, I don't think people will really remember my name. I don't want to be famous. What I want is to be with my family and serve my God." Emily dreaded any change in their lives. Just thinking about change made her feel uncertain. *What if changes made a difference in her and Alex and how close they are? What if this is where the loss would come?*

"Hey I see the worry in your eyes, love. You know that God has not given us the spirit of fear but of a sound mind. Worry comes from the enemy Satan. Remember our devotion that we just read tonight. God is in control and He alone knows and holds the future. Let's trust Him as we have always done."

Emily smiled up at her husband and in her heart she thanked God for him. This man is the only man she had ever loved and she always wanted to be close to him.

As if he read her mind, "I love you my sweet darling, until the end of my days. Nothing could ever change the way I feel about you." Kissing her tenderly he added, "I am yours until death do us part!"

Placing her finger on his lips she spoke quietly as if it was hard to even speak, "Alex never say anything about dying. Please. I love you so much that if you ever died a part of me would die too," She snuggled closer to him as if being closer to him could block out any uncertain feelings about the future.

"It has been a very long and eventful day. Let's go to bed and not think of anything else except loving each other. We can also practice making a tricycle motor." His heart was so full of love for her that his words were almost husky as he picked her up as if she were a small child. She settled into his arms and felt the safety of his presence. They both knew this is where they both belonged. Alex softly caressed her and they were lost in each other's love. In their hearts they were both thanking God for their lives. God had blessed them so much. After making love they drifted off to sleep both feeling satisfied and happy.

Their sleep was peaceful but in the middle of the night Emily began dreaming...

There was rain and lightning. The rain was hard and then she was riding in a pickup truck. She felt fear and something was wrong. The wind was blowing and then she was standing alone staring into a ditch. Alex was lying there and she began screaming, "Alex get up! Please baby get up!"

"Emily, Emily! What's wrong?" Alex was holding her in his arms and she awakened from her dream whimpering, "Alex?" She looked up into his worried face. She was trembling so hard and he was cradling her in his arms making soothing sounds. "Oh Alex, you were..."

"Sh...baby, it was just a bad dream." He caressed her back as he held her held her close.

"I saw you just lying in a ditch in the rain and you weren't moving… you wouldn't get up no matter how I called to you." She sniffled and snuggled closer in his arms.

Alex comforted her and managed to get her calmed down and able to go back to sleep. As they lay there wrapped in each other's arms, he stared into the night. Thoughts of some of Emily's past premonitions filled his mind. When his brother had died, Emily had awakened him insisting that he call Brian. He discovered that Brian was having a heart attack. He had latter died in the hospital. Sometimes, he wondered if he had listened to her, would it have made a difference. When his father had a stroke she had sensed it and called Alex to come home before they ever got the call. She didn't always know what the feelings were-just that they meant something. Maybe it is all coincidence, but now he felt worry flooding his heart and mind about what it all could mean. At the same time he remembered their devotion and knew that the spirit of worry and fear comes from Satan. So he prayed, *Lord I know that you are in control. No matter what this may or may not mean, I trust your presence. Please give her comfort and peace that only You can give. Lord if it is my time to go then let me live each day serving you and taking care of her and the girls.* Alex felt comforted after he prayed and as he closed his eyes to sleep, he thought, *I'll just stay out of the rain!*

The pace began to slow Robyn and Emily busied themselves completing the orders and making their own outfits. Emily had designed and made suits and clothes for Mark and Alex and the children also. After the last gown was finished and picked up, they had a couple of days to prepare for the awards ceremonies. Larry and Kate and the girls had flown in to go with them to visit her parents after the awards. Mark and Robyn's children were there with Robyn's Mom. They too had new clothes to wear to the awards. Larry and Kate would also accompany them to the awards. Kate couldn't believe how beautiful her dress was. Everyone was caught up in the excitement. Alex and Emily were looking forward to going home; the thought of going home was more exciting to them than the awards!

As Robyn and Mark were getting ready for the night's events, Robyn was hoping that Mark would be happy staying home for a while. If he won the award, maybe that would give him enough satisfaction to last for a few months-maybe a year. She understood how much he loved his work, so she tried to be understanding and supportive. Often though, this life style was so uncomfortable for her. Mark had been more relaxed lately and she felt it was because of their friendship with Alex and Emily. He was so much calmer and seemed to truly enjoy her and the family now. A worry that once in this part of his work he would revert to his old self had not materialized. She felt that he too missed home. She stopped and placed a hand on her stomach and spoke to the little one growing inside of her. "I think this will be a good time for you to be born."

She had told Mark last night, "Mark do you think we should have more children?"

"You know I have always said that we should have as many as God wants us to have,"

"Well how do you feel about having one in the near future?"

Mark looked at her grinning he jokingly said, "It might be fun! Want to' get started now?" Grabbing her and kissing her.

"Mark I am serious!" She laughed.

He replied, "Oh I am very serious!"

"How about in a few months?" She smiled at him.

He looked at her and then patted her stomach, "You mean... you are..."

They laughed and then he hugged her, "I love you Mrs. Garrett. You have given me so much of yourself including all of our children. I thank God for you."

"I can't wait to tell Emily. We can make baby clothes and buy material and she is going to teach me how to knit and crochet." Robyn was excitedly making plans.

Mark paused and held up his hand for her to wait, "I don't think we should tell them right away. Alex said they had been trying but weren't having any luck. I think Emily will want to know...just maybe not right now." "

"Emily had mentioned once to me that they were trying, but I didn't think it was really a priority with her. I agree it might put a damper on everything. I can wait until we are home."

"Maybe she is more disappointed than she lets on about it. It could be a bit uncomfortable for her."

Robyn wanted to share this with Emily, but knew Mark had always had a better insight to people than she had. Upon his advice she decided to wait. "Well you are usually right. But don't let that go to your head!"

"Who knows by the time we get home, she might be pregnant too." He crossed over to Robyn and put his arms around her. Then he patted her stomach and kissed her, "I never cease to be amazed when our love makes a child."

At breakfast they were all talking excitedly about the day. Everyone was making plans about where to go and what to do to get ready. The children were just as excited but more about what they would do, than going to the awards.

Alex spoke up, "Why don't you and your family go with us to see Emily's parents? We are leaving tomorrow to spend a few days there. Then we will go home from there."

"I would love to show you my home town. It is a very nice place and it would be fun."

Emily added. She was having a feeling again but not quite sure what it was.

"What do you say?" Alex asked.

"A small town would be great after this place has been this week." Mark looked at Robyn questioning.

That is when the feeling Emily had been having hit her and she smiled and said, "But of course you will need plenty of rest and care in your condition."

Mark shot a look at Robyn; he couldn't believe that Robyn told Emily after their talk last night. "You said you wouldn't say anything to her yet." To his amazement he saw the shock on Robyn's face as she said defensively, "I didn't."

"How did you know, Emily?" Robyn asked.

Alex was grinning as he interjected, "I told you that she reads minds!" He remembered Emily's dream and although this was a happy time he marveled again with amazement at his wife's insight. M a r k and Robyn were speechless and had heard Alex joke about her foresight, and now they had seen it firsthand. Mark had witnessed her perceptive ability to think on her feet, but this was incredible.

Emily embarrassed by the focus on her, attempted to change the subject. "I think this is wonderful and a much needed event to slow things down."

"That is what I want too. Best of all I can now share it with my very best friends."

"We just wanted to wait because we knew you guys were trying and we didn't want things to be awkward between us." Mark explained.

"Emily and I have decided that for now whatever reasons God has we were just going to leave it up to Him as to when or if we have another child." Alex smiled and then rubbed his hands together, "Oh well for now we plan to spoil your baby!" They laughed as Emily hugged Robyn and Alex shook Mark's hand.

The day went fast it seemed it was filled with crowds of people-meeting new people and speaking with people with whom they had recently became acquainted. Mark had won the award and she had been recognized for her designs. After an interview with a magazine, she had an invitation by a famous store to sell her dresses, Emily felt drained by the pace of everything. She was already making outfits in her mind for the new baby.

They left the next morning and once they were back in Arkansas, Emily enjoyed introducing Robyn and Mark to all her friends and family. They had started dropping by the hotel where they were staying almost immediately. The church gave them a party and it was very nice, but things were different. She realized that this was a place to visit now and her home was in Australia. When she showed the Garretts their old home place they were amazed that it was so small. Emily found herself missing her home and wishing for the day for them to return-to Australia.

The day finally arrived when they began the journey home. Emily felt so glad when they boarded the last flight that would take them home. She settled back and fell asleep. Once they arrived it was so good to finally be home and that night after devotions and prayers they climbed into their own bed. The next morning just before sunrise, Emily slipped quietly out of bed and made her way down to the kitchen. She took time to read the Word and pray. Kate had entered the kitchen and was preparing breakfast. Emily smiled at her and hugged her as then poured herself some coffee.

"I figured you would be up because sunrise is about to begin." Kate grinned.

Emily hugged her again and said, "It is so good to be home. You have my schedule pegged."

She took her cup and went out to the porch to watch the sun come up. Kate had learned her routine and she realized how much she missed having her around. Looking down at the porch swing, she saw that Kate had already placed a blanket there for her in case the morning was chilly. As the golden rays of sunlight shot its beautiful light into the new day, everything became clearer. The greens of the land were sharper and the blue of the sky was brilliant. Alex came up beside her and put his arm around her, "I thought I would find you here." His heart was filled with a great love for her. He had waited for her to have her time, but today he felt that he needed to be near her, as he was painfully aware that his life would be endlessly empty without her.

"It is so beautiful isn't it? I think this is my favorite part of the day." Emily smiled up at him.

"You are beautiful." He reached down and stroked her hair. She was tiny but such an important part of his existence. "It sure is good to be home."

"This is home, and I realized it more when I missed being here. I couldn't wait to get here." Emily explained, "I miss my family and friends back in Arkansas, but this place is such a part of me. Mark and Robyn have become family too." She sat down on the swing with Alex seated beside her, he spread the blanket over them both.

"Speaking of Mark and Robyn, I would like to do something special for their baby."

"I am making a layette and quilt for it. I know what you can do. Remember those little horses that you made for the girls when they were little? You did such a good job on those."

"You always know just what people need. I watched you and how you dealt with the people on the set. Not only did you know what needed to be done, but also how to build up those who needed encouragement." He put his arm around her shoulders. "I am so proud of you. You were so great with everyone. Mark was so surprised how well you perceived their needs."

"Really? Well it was hard work but it was fun. Still it is great to be home."

"Yes it is Em."

She had once thought she would never feel at home in this place, but the last year and half had gone so quickly since she first met the Garrets. Their friendship had grown and she now felt as if they were family. The Garretts had become an important part of their life. She felt a bond with them more than she had felt with any of her other friends. On the day she met them she had no idea how close the two families would become. Alex and Mark were as close as brothers and the children also had bonded with each other. Emily didn't understand but somehow she knew they were all meant to be together. Is this why God brought them here? She often questioned God but he always gave her peace. God always knows and sometimes although it is hard; she knew she needed to trust that His plan is to work things out His way.

Her mind shifted to her daughter, Leigha hurriedly finishing her chores so she could ride off to meet Hank. They were young, but Emily had been young when she fell in love with Alex. They had talked to her about the appropriate things to do and to know that she has a duty to be what God wants her to be. She and Alex had shown them the benefits of always doing and being what God wants us to be. She truly trusted her children.

Smiling to herself she thought how they would spend hours riding horses. Alex would tell them they needed to let the horses rest. They knew how to take care of the horses and both children were very responsible. Erika, Edward and Nancy were always together also. They loved fishing, gardening and painting. Often they would get their fishing gear and go down to the pond to fish. Edward was also quite the photographer and carried his camera everywhere they went. Robyn had taught him how to develop his film. Erika, Nancy and Edward had designed and were busy filling a photo album of their adventures. Ariel, Wesley, and Louis spent endless hours in the tree house that Alex and Mark had built. They played house and had make believe adventures. They all played well together. It seemed that they were always here or at Mark and Robyn's house.

They were all busy making Christmas gifts. Emily's parents were flying down for Christmas. Her Dad had visited Australia when he was in the Navy. Her Mom had never been out of the states so she was very excited. Dad had visited several of the pacific islands and he had been to India and Israel on missionary trips. Mom was looking forward to spending time with the girls. Her favorite was Ariel although she insisted that she didn't have favorites, Emily knew that Ariel would get her full attention. From the time Ariel had been little she had followed her Grandmother around the house. She always wanted to learn how to do things. Ariel had a grace and beauty all her own. She was the shiest of the three girls. She had always been more serious and loving than the others. Whenever anyone asked her what she wanted to be when she grew up, the answer was always 'A Mommy!' She was close to Wesley and Louis and the three were inseparable.

Her thoughts were spastically entering her mind. It was like every thought she had not had time to think about over the last few weeks, were waiting in line to be considered next. For a long time she sat considering all the thoughts, she realized she had kept busy not allowing herself to do any deep thinking. She was always afraid the dark feeling about Alex would return if she allowed her mind to go there. Her dream had reoccurred several times and each time more was revealed. Each time she always prayed, *"God please don't let this happen."* She shook her head and scolded to herself. *"Stop this silly nonsense! It is just a dream!"*

She and Alex had been sitting quietly watching the children play and sipping coffee. Alex noticed a deep frown on her face. "What is the matter?"

Startled from her thoughts by the sound of his voice, she jumped a little. Trying to make light of the situation she remarked laughing, "Oh I just ran out of space in my mind and didn't know where to go."

Knowing that look and having seen it before he knew she was trying to be funny to cover up what she was feeling. He knew that she would share with him when she was ready. "Let's go for a walk, I know when I have been shut out!" He got up and pulled her to her feet.

"A walk sounds good. We can plan what we will do when my parents come."

They walked down the road and talked as they went, "Is that what you were worried about?"

"You can always read my face." She playfully shoved him. But he knew that she had once again avoided a direct answer to his question. Deciding to go along with her thoughts he said, "I can't wait for them to see this place. I think they will see how blessed and happy we are here. Does the next eight years seem like a long time?"

"At first I dreaded it, but now I can't imagine living anywhere else. When we were back in the states all I could think about was getting back here."

"I think I was made for this life. I love ranching and I am looking forward to business trips for the family advertising business." He reached down and picked her up and carried her over to the fence. "We can bring any of our family here any time." He sat her on the fence and continued, "I was thinking that maybe Lynette and John and their children, Steve, Deb, and Michael, could come too."

"It would be nice to have your sister here. I have missed them." Emily agreed,

"That was one of the reasons for this walk, because I wanted to ask you about bringing them down. John traveled some in the service, but Lynette has never been out of the states. It would be fun…You just keep doing it!" Alex shook his head in amazement.

"Don't exaggerate honey, sometimes I just get lucky!"

As Alex was lifting her down from the fence, Emily noticed a rider coming fast. It was Hank and Emily sensed something wrong.

"Alex! Alex! Please Dad needs you. One of our cattle is in trouble. He needs you to bring your come-along. His foreman has gone into town to get the vet."

"I will get the jeep and head on over." You rest your horse and go in and get yourself something to drink."

Emily had him sit down on the porch while she went in to get him a drink. Leigha was coming down the stairs. "Hey, Mom can I go see Hank? We are planning a surprise for Grandpa and Grandma and it takes a lot of work."

"I don't see why not. Just go out on the porch, and take this with you when you go and give it to the guy sitting out there." Smiling impishly handing Leigha a cup of water.

Once outside Leigha noticed Hank and said, "I was just going to see if I could come over to your house."

"We had some problems with one of the cows. Alex is on his way over. I rode my horse and it's resting now."

As the two sat talking, Emily was so glad that her kids were here and that she wasn't going to have to worry about them being in the wrong crowd or getting mixed up with drugs. One thing about Hank and Leigha all they had on their minds was horses.

Alex spent most of the day at Mark's. She took a picnic lunch over and a change of clothes for Alex. Emily's thoughts were centered on the day and praying that their friendship would be a long happy one.

CHAPTER
SIX

~

Christmas was approaching fast and although the preparations were all finished and ready, Emily was excited and restlessly awaiting the family's arrival. Her parents, Alex's sister and family, were all coming for the holidays to spend two weeks with them. Alex commented that she was getting hard to control because she kept wondering when they all would get there.

Her parents, Lynette and John along with their children Debra, Michael, and Steve, were arriving in a few days. Steve's new bride Brandi was coming as well. Emily wanted a full house and the decorations for the season were up and everything looked very festive. She wondered how they would feel about having a warm Christmas. She wanted everyone especially her father to know she had accepted her new home. At first her father had known she was unhappy and lonely, but now Emily wanted her family to see how happy she felt. She had wished her parents would join her here, at least when he is ready to retire.

"Can I interrupt your deep thoughts?" Alex entered the room.

Emily jumped and turned around to face him, "Alex! You scared me! I thought you were still outside. Did you finish decorating the barn?"

"Obviously you are not very sharp today. I have been through and even taken a shower."

He grinned and hugged her, "See I even smell good!"

"Yes you are rather smelly." Emily teased. "Kind of sexy too." Alex flexed his muscles and winked at her. "Well, Mr. America," she punched him playfully, "How about a date?"

"I just don't know about that …I have seen your husband and I don't think I want to tangle with that dude."

"We could slip in a few minutes before he gets home. That is if you are interested."

Alex pulled her close as he thanked God for her. He hadn't always been sure that she would stay with him now he was sure that they would be together forever. As he held her a bit tighter Emily became aware that he was also deep in thought. "Alex what are you thinking about?" He kissed her gently, not being very good with words or explaining his feelings he simply replied, "Just about how much I love you."

"I love you too. The smartest thing I ever did was to take you my handsome hunk off the market. Especially before that Taylor person got her meat hooks in you!" She smiled knowingly that her husband had difficulty often expressing his feelings.

"Took me right out of her hands, did ya' sweetheart,"

"Just like that." She snapped her fingers.

"Give me a break; you know she was never my type. She did give me a bit of advice."

"What would that be?"

"She said that you would never be happy with me because you were just a baby and once the newness of having an older man wore off, you would move on."

"Goes to show you, that she wasn't very smart." Playfully folding her arms, "Maybe I will send her a Christmas card, just to let her know that I still find you very sexy! I could send her our Christmas picture."

She playfully shoved him and started to walk away. He quickly grabbed her and was pretending to keep her from getting away. She laughed and said, "Who knows maybe in a few years I will trade you in on a younger model."

Suddenly they heard Mark clearing his throat. Mark had been watching the scene and almost envying the closeness they obviously shared. Although he envied them it is their love for each other had inspired him and Robyn to become closer. He was grinning at their horse playing, "Caught you two goofing off!" Mark joined the fun, "I thought if I stood around long enough I could get a tidbit of information to hold over your head."

Emily blushed as Alex returned her to the floor and released his hold on her. "Mark is everyone here already?" Alex had invited the Garrett's to join the family.

"I need to ask you something," Mark said. "Hank and Leigha are riding their horses in the Christmas parade and the other children want to create a nativity scene on my flatbed trailor. Could Larry pull it with your tractor?"

"That would be fantastic!" Emily bubbled with excitement. "What a wonderful way to show my family how wonderful this town is." Turning to Alex by the expression of amuzement on his face she had the feeling he already knew all about this.

Mark called down the hallway, "We have the Emily seal of approval."

The children and Robyn came rushing into the room, hugging every one as they excitedly commented happily. Emily stood back and watched the scene as she realized that Mark and Robyn were largely responsible for the way she felt now. Their friendship had bonded her to this place as no other thing could have.

Mark noticing how happy Emily looked lifted his hands for everyone to be quiet, "Okay everybody we have one more thing to ask Emily."

"Of course I will do the costumes. Between Robyn and me, we can turn them out in no time."

Mark just shook his head, her insight was uncanny. "What can I say I am a push over for a bunch of kids? Thanks Emily."

"Well since we only have a few days we need to get started on the plans. Let's start by measuring the flatbed and getting materials together." Alex jumped in to manager mode.

Walking into the kitchen, Emily turned to Robyn who was very pale with a pained look on her face." Turning to Robyn and having her sit in a chair she called out to Kate. "Kate come quickly!"

"Emily it is just this pregnancy it has been the worse pregnancy I have ever had. I just can't keep anything down at all."

"I will fix you some of my peppermint tea." Kate offered. "It has always helped me."

After fixing the tea she brought it over to Robyn.

"I don't think I can drink anything."

"Just try a few sips to start. Put your feet up here on the ottoman. Just take it slow and let it do the work."

"Here Robyn, relax and rest for a while." Emily comforted her friend.

After a few minutes the color returned to Robyn's face and she obvious was feeling better. Kate brought her a few crackers to munch. They went into the sewing room and Emily settled her down in the big lounge chair in the room. Robyn smiled at her friend and felt so grateful that she was there for her.

Emily once assured that Robyn was fine, returned to sewing mode, "I made Hank and Leigha matching outfits and they are riding with another group of riders. Emily held up the two carefully crafted outfits, both in a pretty blue. There was a beautifully embroidered design on both the shirts and the pants. She then brought out the matching boots and Robyn could see the embroidery on the outfits matched the designs on the boots.

"This is why I asked for Hank's boot size. This is the first time I ever made outfits to match shoes." Emily laughed. Alex bought the matching boots and hats too." She showed her the outfits. "I also made the hatbands for the hats."

"They will be the best-dressed riders in the whole parade."

It was at that moment that Robyn wondered how Emily knew to make outfits. "Did Leigha mention the parade to you?"

"Actually this is the first time I heard about it. I am not sure why I made the outfits, but they just seemed to be something I wanted to do."

"How did you know?" Robyn asked.

"Just my intuition I guess." Emily hating it when people noticed her gift. "Well I guess we have a great deal of work to do. Let's get cracking. My family will be here soon but I want to get some things ready before they get here."

Robyn sensed that the subject was closed. Although she would love to know more, she respected her friend so she stopped asking questions. They worked hard over the next few days; the guys were building and the ladies sewing. Also they spent family time in the evenings playing, singing, reading the Bible. They grilled hamburgers, went on picnics, and lounged around the pool. Each experience bonded the two families closer. It seemed they were more than friends. They seemed more like family.

Leigha and Hank were growing closer each day. They were always together and always sought each other out wherever they went. The day for the parade was drawing closer. Tomorrow their family would arrive and Emily was very excited. The weather would be warmer than they were used to having, but the festivities and decorations showed the season. Larry, Alex and Mark had gone into Sydney for a business trip a few days ago and stayed to pick up the families when they arrived.

Robyn and her children were staying with Emily because Mark didn't want Robyn to be alone at this time. Robyn was better but had been experiencing spells of weakness. Her doctor insisted that things would get better and gave her more vitamins. He blamed her weakness on the fact she had trouble keeping food down. Emily had mixed feelings about the whole situation. She was trying hard to block the dark feelings she had about it, but often tiptoed into Robyn's room at night to check on her, before she felt comfortable to go to bed herself.

"God please let everything go alright." Emily prayed. As she drifted off to sleep, *her dreams were filled with people running in and out of her bedroom -some laughing and some solemn. She was with Alex and Robyn both smiling. So she slipped deeper into a peaceful sleep. But just before dawn she dreamed again, this time she, Alex, and Mark were crying and then they were happy. Suddenly it was only she and Mark and they were crying and then just as suddenly they were happy again.* Upon awakening Emily felt confused at first but then the dream soon faded from her memory. "Strange dream, whatever it meant." She got ready and hurried downstairs, to spend her time with God. Bible study and prayer time was the best beginning of each day. Then she loved sitting on her porch and watching the sunrise. It was this time of the day when she felt the closeness of her Lord and Savior.

"God if it's your will let everything work out for the good. I know that You know what is best for my life, so please help me to always remember to rely on You always. I love you Jesus and I thank you for always taking care of me."

In the mornings she felt like Jesus was standing beside her, *"Lord, be my guide and thank you so much for your sacrifice for my sins. You have done so much for me."* Momentarily her mind flickered to the disturbing dreams she had been having. *"Please help me to be patient to understand the dreams. I don't know why you chose to give me these foresights or even if they are insights. Everything You do is for a purpose and I know that eventually You will show me Your wisdom. Help me to see what you want me to see and to always follow Your way. More than any other thing I want my walk to be with You and to do only that which is Your will. Thank you so much for my family and friends. I know that I could not face life without You by my side. Happy birthday Jesus."*

She decided to open the drapes in the front of the house so it would be bright and cheerful when the children awakened. Just as she finished she heard a car coming up the driveway. Opening the door she saw a car pull up to the door. Mark hopped out and then her parents exited. As she ran out to meet them Mark was saying, "I told you that she would be up and waiting. No one can fool her."

"Actually I am surprised!" Everyone was hugging happily.

Mom was saying, "It is so big and beautiful."

Dad added, "It is bigger than I remembered it."

"Wait until you see the inside." As she took her Mom's hand she shot a look at Mark.   "Where's Alex?"

"They will be here soon. His sister was a bit airsick so they are letting her get her land legs. How's ..?"

"She is sleeping and doing fine. Her night was peaceful. I get up early for my quiet time with God."

Mark always admired her closeness to God. He often wondered if he could ever be that close to God. She really is something Mark was thinking as they entered the house. Everyone was talking and laughing at once. Emily was telling her parents that she would get the kids up and they could have breakfast and then show them around. "When Alex gets here he can show you around the property."

"Grandma and Grandpa!" Ariel bounded down the stairs and grabbed first Grandma then Grandpa. "I have missed you so much." Lois and Wesley were not far behind her. They ran over to Mark and hugged him. "Hi, Dad." Then they hugged the McLeods. Hank and Leigha entered next and as they were hugging everyone Nancy, Erika, and Edward came down the stairs. Everyone took turns hugging each other.

Emily looked at Mark who had a worried look on his face. She quietly went up the stairs while everyone was talking. Mark watched her go and knew she had sensed his worry. *'She always knows! It's like she is in my head."* He thought to himself. Mark got up and followed her up the stairs.

Emily had checked on Robyn and found her resting peacefully. As she was coming from the room she saw Mark coming toward her, "She is still asleep and resting nicely."

"She is usually up by now," Mark glanced worriedly toward her room.

"She's pregnant and she knows that the kids are in good hands. She has had a rough time of this lately. I think a restful sleep will do her good."

"She never had any trouble carrying our other children. I am worried."

Noticing the quiver in Mark's voice, Emily asked, "What does her doctor say?"

"He just thinks she is having a tougher time because she is older and it has been over six years since her last birth. He keeps saying things will get better, but I am worried because everything is getting worse." Mark paused to gain control of his emotions, "She is more tired lately and she has never had morning sickness that lasted this long. I feel so helpless."

"Mark we need to pray and be extra strong for her." They bowed their heads and prayed.

"Just remember, Mark, God is always there. You need to trust Him and talk to Him."

Mark reached out touched her hand, "Alex gave me the same advice. It's time I listened to it." He stepped back and smiled, "God sent you two here you know. We needed your leadership."

"Well now that's funny because I felt like God sent you to me as well."

"You and Alex have meant so much to us. We have become closer to each other and closer to God as a result of our friendship. As a result all my children have accepted Christ. You both have shown us how important God is to our lives. We love you both."

Emily was blushing, praise always made her feel unworthy. "Mark isn't it wonderful how God changes lives? All we have to do is place Him in control and so many lives can be touched by Him if we let Him use us. It isn't Alex or me when all is said it is God alone that changes us."

Mark was amazed and watched her face glow as she spoke about God. He finally knew just how her close relationship with God had developed. *'She gives God every bit of the credit for all the good in her life,'* he thought. He knew that he and Robyn had drawn closer to God through Alex and Emily's influence. He prayed, *"God help me be strong for Robyn."*

They returned to the group downstairs. Robyn woke up later and seemed refreshed. Emily talked them into staying another night. Even though they argued they didn't want to be in the way of their family time. Emily reminded them they were considered family too.

That evening Alex, Lynette, and her family arrived just in time for supper. There were more hugs and loads of excitement. They too were amazed at the size of the house. They had a hasty tour while Kate, Pam, and Becky set up the dining room. After dinner they all gathered in the Library and the girls sang songs. All the children joined in and they sounded very good.

"All this, the house and people to wait on you is unbelievable." Lynette was saying, "It must be heavenly."

"God has been good to us." Alex smiled at his sister. "Now everyone gather around for our nightly devotion."

Her father led the group in a devotional on the story of Joseph and how he stood with God in spite of all that he had to endure. He always had a knack for telling the Bible stories in such a way that even the little ones were attentive. It was clear to Mark and Robyn where Emily got her foundation.

Once baths were over and children tucked safely in bed for the night, the adults sat on the porch taking over the day's events and the plans for the days ahead. Once every couple was in their rooms and settled for the night. She found herself finally with her husband's arms around her. He drew her closer and said, "This is great and it feels so nice to have everyone here."

He looked down at his wife and felt her love shining through her eyes. "I love you Alex."

As usual his attempt to not be too serious he grinned, "Want to make a tricycle motor?"

Emily loved him even though he rarely wanted to be serious. So she joined in, "You know I am not very mechanically inclined and does your wife know that you are making these propositions?"

"No, but I will keep quiet if you will." He crossed over and shut the door then turning around he grabbed her up, threw her over his shoulder, and carried her to the bed. She was giggling, "Now little missy we aren't going to keep this secret if you don't keep quiet. You will wake up the whole house."

Only one person saw them because Mark had quietly opened the door when Alex picked up his wife. He then withdrew just as quietly. He smiled to himself as he went to his room and closed the door.

Alex made love to his wife. She was always amazed at just how tender his touch was. He was a large man with large hands, but his gentleness with her was part of what made their love making so good. Totally satisfied they proclaimed their love to each other and both drifted off to sleep.

Emily awakened from her sleep and reached for Alex only to find him missing. Reaching for her robe she found herself going from room to room and finding no one. She wanted Alex but he was nowhere to be found. There was the sound of crying at the bottom of the stairs. Mark was standing in front of her with his hands reaching out to her. Tears were flowing down his face. She reached out for him and suddenly it wasn't Mark but it was Alex. Then Alex turned and went outside. She followed him, but realized they weren't in the yard, but she was back at the ditch with Alex at the bottom lying beside his truck and it was raining and windy. There was the sound of thunder and she was watching herself jump in the ditch, "Alex wake up! No you can't sleep here. Please get up." She was screaming and a hand lifted her up to her feet. "Come on Em. Let the medics do their job." She looked at the voice and it was Mark. "There isn't anything we can do; he's gone." She saw Mark had tears on his face.

Terror filled her whole body as she sat straight up in her bed. Alex was sleeping peacefully beside her. Although she realized it was only a dream she was trembling. The clock said it was only 4:00 am. She was shaking and sweating so she got up and took a shower. Still unable to shake the dream she dressed and went quietly downstairs. She tried desperately to file it away in her mind. She stopped and read the scripture where God has not given us the spirit of fear, but of a sound mind. Then she read Psalm 23 because it always comforted her. Finding herself going out on the porch, she sank to her knees. Overwhelmed by the realistic dream, with a heavy heart she prayed, *"God I don't understand and truthfully I don't think I want to understand. I haven't dreamed this dream in so long why now? We are so happy and this is a happy time. Lord I have always tried not to question You about anything. I try to accept Your will. But please don't take Alex. Not Alex. Please!"* She gulped for air as she made her petition known to God. *"I'm sorry, Lord. I know Your ways are best and only You know the future. But God I can't live without him. How could I ever be happy again? He is the only man I have ever loved."* She slumped and placed her head in her hands as the tears flooded her face. A chair sliding across the porch brought her to the present. She jerked her head up to see Mark coming toward her. At first she thought she was still dreaming.

"I am really sorry, I didn't mean to intrude. I saw you pass our door and you looked very upset. I didn't intend to listen but is there something wrong with Alex?" He reached down to help her to her feet. "I heard you ask God not to take him. I didn't mean to listen to your prayer,

But you looked so upset." As Mark lifted her he felt her trembling. "Hey you are all shook up." He gently sat her down in the chair.

"Oh, Mark I didn't want to wake anyone. I just had a bad dream and it was so real."

She dabbed her eyes trying to regain her composure. "I needed to pray. Sometimes when I dream it seems real and I guess it just got to me."

"Just sit here and if you want to talk I will listen." Mark patted her shoulder comfortingly. He had a feeling that there was more to this than just a bad dream. He pulled up another chair and sat down. "If I can help I would like to do that."

She wanted to talk and she needed to talk, but it was as if she put the dream into words it would become real. No she thought I need to keep this to myself. "Mark, thank you…but I can't talk about it. It is all so hard to deal with…" A look of sheer terror covered her face once more. Somehow Mark and Robyn were part of it and she didn't dare share it. She looked at Mark, "You and Robyn were in it too. Maybe that means that you'll be here when…" She jumped up and faced Mark realizing that she almost put losing Alex into words. Turning suddenly to go she felt as if the world was closing in on her. "Mark!" Then darkness overtook her.

Mark caught her as she fainted. He lifted her small body and was amazed at the lightness of her. He carried her inside to a lounge chair and ran to get a cold rag. He placed it on her head and she began to move, "Lie still and don't move." He wanted to go for Alex but was afraid to leave her.

"I am okay. Mark." Emily still felt disoriented so she chose to stay in the chair.

"Stay right there. I will be right back."

Mark ran up the stairs into Alex's room and over to his bed. "Hey, big guy wake up. It's Emily she's downstairs. Come on get up."

"Okay man I am awake. What's wrong?" He questioned while reaching for his robe.

As they descended the stairs, "She fainted! She's in the lounge chair now."

Alex sped up as they hurried down the stairs. Mark told Alex that she had a bad dream and he came out on the porch to hear her begging God not to take him. Alex knew that Mark didn't understand how real Emily's dreams could be. Alex was reminded once again that his days could be numbered. As they went toward the room, Mark noticed the look on Alex's face. "Hey man are you okay? You aren't keeping things from me are you? I know we are only friends but you are like a brother to me. You would tell me if…"

Alex shook his head and broke in to Mark's inquiry, "There isn't anything wrong that I know of. After all it is Emily's dream." He shrugged his shoulders trying to sooth the situation and said, "It's hard to explain."

Once in the room, Alex reached down and picked her up and sat down with her in his lap. He held her as if she were a small child and comforted her as she cried softly into his shoulder. Mark stood back and silently watched as Alex spoke softly and stroked her hair. He marveled at the bond they shared. It seemed they both always knew just what the other one needed. He felt that he shared in that bond because they had all become a family. This relationship was from God and a gift he would forever be thankful that God had brought them into their lives.

Mark's thoughts were interrupted by a touch on his shoulder, "Robyn." He placed his finger on his lips and led her to the porch. He quietly explained what had taken place.

"I thought that possibly something was wrong, when you got up and didn't return."

"Robyn, I know this all means that we all belong together as family. I can't explain it but I think our lives were intertwined from the beginning. Alex is the brother I always wanted."

"I know; I feel the same way. Do you think Emily will be okay? She takes such good care of me. I wonder if she has had other dreams. What was it about anyway?"

"I don't know for sure what it was, but from Alex's reaction, I have the feeling she had it before, because he knew about it. It was something about losing Alex. She wouldn't elaborate, but she did say we were in it too. But what shook me to the bone was the sheer terror on her face. I saw her face as she went by our room so I got dressed and went down to check on her. Whatever it was it tore her heart out."

They were standing hand in hand watching the sun rise. He reached around her and patted her stomach. They were smiling as Alex and Emily joined them, apologizing for the drama.

"Sometimes my dreams get the best of me. Now you both know my weakness. It is this big guy." She playfully poked Alex on his chest. The mood was changed and suddenly Mark's hand jumped and he grinned at his wife "I think I just got kicked." Everyone was laughing. Emily breathed a sigh of relief as she realized that she had once again avoided sharing the haunting dream.

"I am starving." Robyn smiled.

Mark grinned "That sounds great."

They all went in to see if Kate was up yet. She had become accustomed to Emily and Alex both being early risers. She had coffee ready when they entered the kitchen.

"Well I am used to Emily being up early and Alex shortly after that, but it looks like a convention this morning."

"Robyn is hungry." Emily smiled.

"That sounds great. I will make you some toast but don't overdo just yet."

"Kate you have taken such good care of me and I truly thank you so much."

Every one discussed the events that were to take place that day as they drank coffee. Kate prepared breakfast and soon the rest of the household began gathering around the dining table. There was so much joy and love in the room, adding more excitement to the coming parade.

Once at the parade it proved to be a day everyone would cherish. Emily could see the pride in her parent's eyes as they watched their grandchildren pass by. Little Ariel who was one of the shepherds yelled "Hi Grandma and Grandpa." Robyn and Mark's kids had already accepted Emily's parents as grandparents and they were waving excitedly too. Lynette's children had also taken part in the parade. Edward was busy taking photos of everyone. He was dressed as a shepherd, but was busy jumping on and off the float. Alex noticed Michael and Erika holding hands and poked Emily in the ribs with is elbow, to get her to notice them. He whispered, "Did the shepherds hold hands." Looking into his handsome face she saw his boyish grin and a twinkle in his blue grey eyes. She knew that she was truly blest with this man. Love had blessed her whole life. She had loving parents who introduced her to the Lord and raised her in a Christian home. Alex had given her three lovely children. His sister and her family were a blessing and now her new family Robyn and Mark.

After the parade they all gathered for a good old fashioned cookout. "This is a lot better than cold weather." Her dad remarked.

"Well Dad you could stay here every Christmas."

"We do have plenty of room!" Ariel chimed in.

"Well I still have a few good years left before I retire." Her dad reminded her.

"Oh Daddy, You know I am just selfish but I want you close by."

"Well everyone we have clean suits in the pool house. Who wants to swim?" Alex asked.

Everyone except Emily and Lynette went for a swim. Lynette and Emily took a walk down the driveway. It was the first real chance they had to be alone. Emily seeking to put Lynette at ease, "What do you think about the place?"

It is fantastic. I was so overwhelmed at the size of it. I expected big from your letters, but I never expected an estate. All this land and the responsibilities must be stupendous. Alex tells me that you have a business in Sydney too."

"Yes but Alex is handling that. At first all I did was try to stay busy, but I was very sad."

"I could tell in your letters, that you were unhappy. But then it all changed. You actually got a mention at the awards for your designs."

"When I met the Garretts I learned to accept it all and then I came to think of it as home. I stopped waiting for the ten years to be over. I truly am home. Alex was so amazing; how quickly he adapted to everything is wonderful. It was like this had always been his life. He runs the place like he was born here. My uncle's businesses are prospering and Alex is just as at home in the office as he is here. Our lawyer, friend, and advisor, Richard Palmer, is training him in the business"

Emily was trying to ease Lynette but she had a feeling of desperation coming from her sister-in-law. The feeling Emily was getting from her was unbearable. Lynette was smiling and talking but once Emily homed in on a feeling from someone close to her, she couldn't shake it. Finally she had to speak up, "Lynette, I have never been one to beat around the bush and you know that. So I am ending the small talk, out with it."

"Em I didn't want to put a damper on the holidays. Everything here is so perfect." Emily stomped her foot and put her hands on her hips. So Lynette knew she had to finish what she started. "John didn't get his promotion and they are cutting his job. When Alex asked us to come it was like at least we would have a good vacation before we had to tighten our belts."

"You know you could always come here and work for Alex."

"We couldn't leave Steve especially since they are just starting out. He just started a new position at his company. John's parents are in poor health so he needs to stay close to home. Plus John wouldn't want to leave."

"Let's just pray about this and let God handle it. He will let us know the solution."

They prayed together and Lynette hugged her and said she felt much better.

"Now let's go enjoy the Australian weather. It isn't always you get to visit another country for Christmas."

"You know you helped and I should have known that I wouldn't be able to keep anything from you. By the way I do feel better."

"Good, I believe with all my heart that leaving things in God's hands always makes it better."

They headed back and Lynette missed the twinkle in Emily's eye as they turned to leave. The next morning Robyn and Mark came early. They celebrated Christmas and Emily enjoyed giving her presents to everyone. Both handmade and money gifts were appreciated. Emily especially enjoyed the photo album that the kids had made. Some pictures she had seen or was there when they were taken, but they had so many that she hadn't seen. Everyone was laughing and have a good time. Lynette and John were shocked when they found that their money envelops included a thousand dollars each. She had given her parents the same thing and each child a hundred along with each handmade gift. The children left the room and went upstairs to play. Emily was so glad that she could give them all something good.

At the end of the day she sat on the porch watching the sunset. She dreaded tomorrow when everyone had to leave. She wished they could all just stay. She knew that she could visit them but she wanted them close.

As the sun sank lower in the sky, and the sky began to darken but Emily was unaware of the darkening shadows as she remembered the joy and happiness of the day. In her mind she cherished each smile and each face. She knew that Alex had enjoyed helping John and Lynette and she also knew the only way they would accept money is if it was a gift. She smiled as she thought of them.

Alex was standing in the shadows watching her. Seeing her smile, he cleared his throat and said, "Hey cutie how's about a date?" He lifted her to her feet and hugged her. "It's my turn to see all and know all. Let me see you are wishing everyone would just move in."

"Hey that's pretty good. My love you are so right."

"Em, I tried to talk John in to taking a position at our company in Sydney, but he won't leave the states. His job has been eliminated and the company has sold out to another company. Sounds familiar doesn't it. He agreed to take some money but didn't want to tell Lynette until after Christmas was over. I reminded him of all the times they helped us so he was a bit more accepting."

"Maybe this is why God gave us all this money, so we could help others." Emily smiled.

"Well, I have another surprise for you, Mark had a company in Little Rock and he is hiring him to take over there. It was a part of his inheritance. He wasn't sure what he would do but now he is happy because he has someone he can trust. It is something that John knows how to do."

"Have you told John?"

"No, Mark is coming over tomorrow to tell him."

"Thanks you are fantastic." She laughed and he said you better save one of those hugs for Mark. "But for now you want to go upstairs?" He grinned and took her hand and together they went up to bed. Everyone had already turned in because they had an early day tomorrow.

The morning came all too quickly, and as they were packing the cars, Mark drove up.

Emily could barely hold her joy. Alex had taken John and Lynette into the library, "Here is a check for all the money that you have given us over the years when we needed help. I won't take no for an answer."

"Thank you Alex. This will pay off our bills and give us a little to live on until I find another position." As John shook Alex's hand Emily and Mark entered the room.

"Hey guys how are you doing?" Mark greeted them. "John, I have a company in Little Rock and I need someone with your talents to oversee it so that I can keep it open. If you are interested the job is yours. Here is the salary and job description. I have already contacted them and they are expecting you to come in when you get back home."

Lynette was crying softly and John was so surprised. They would not even have to move from their home in Bryant. He shook Mark's hand and thanked him for the job. They all were happy as they left for a side trip to Melbourne before going on to Sydney to fly back. They did some sight-seeing and then the next morning they left for Sydney. After everyone left they checked into a hotel and as Emily sat looking out the window she thought about how great it had been to have her family there. Her mom and dad had always been there for her when she had a crisis and now they were far away. *"God please send me someone to help me through all of this. Help me stay strong. Please don't take Alex."*

She looked at the garden below and decided to go for a walk. She left Alex a note and made her way down to the lobby. Mark saw her and went out to talk to her. Once again he walked up on her as she was praying. "Lord please not Alex, I can't face that alone. I know you don't make mistakes and that you are always right. Please." She bowed her head and tears ran down her cheeks. Mark stood there helpless and ashamed that he had once again intruded on her privacy. He wanted to comfort her, Instead he quietly turned and went back inside.

Emily lifted her head and spoke aloud, "I am not sure what is going to happen, but these dreams are telling me that I will need every bit of faith that I possess. Help me Lord." Just then the verse from Philippians came to her mind, "I can do all things through Christ, who strengthens me." She smiled and said "Yes Thank you Lord."

Mark noticed Emily as she entered the hotel. She had a peaceful look on her face. He marveled at how she always found peace. "*God help me find that peace. She came out to find peace and found you waiting there. Help may faith grow stronger and give me your strength.*"

Emily saw Mark and crossed over to him. "Hi I was just walking in the garden."

"I was just going for a walk."

"It is a nice night. I always feel closer to God when I am outside. Enjoy your walk, Mark. See you in the morning."

Mark waved as she got on the elevator. As he went outside, he looked toward heaven and wondered what the future held for both the Garretts and the Daniels.

CHAPTER
SEVEN

Once again the family found themselves in a period of anticipation. They had been busy decorating the nursery for Robyn's upcoming pregnancy. Closeness in the relationship brought them always together doing something. The bond between the two families had grown and developed into an unbreakable family bond.

"Robyn do you really think it is wise to go to Sydney now?" Emily worried.

"I am fine Mrs. Worry Pants," she grinned at Emily, "Mark is too sick to go and someone has to handle the business."

"Okay but you need to hurry and finish your business and get home as soon as you have completed it."

"Yes of course! Mother!" They both laughed.

"I did sound a bit pushy, didn't I?"

"More like bossy I'd say."

They had laughed and joked around, "Well Emily what are friends for? If you didn't tell me Mark would."

After Emily left for home Robyn went upstairs to check on Mark who was in bed. "How's that fever?" She checked his fever and kissed his forehead.

"It is better, my love." Mark said, "I wish that you would let Alex go. He knows the business, as well as I do. After all he can still see his toes." His laugh turned to a cough. He laid back on his pillow in apparent misery.

"See, you make a jab at me and you pay!" She grinned and then gave him a dose of cough medicine. The worried look on his face made her stop momentarily. "I know that you are worried but Emily and Kate have taken good care of me and I feel much better."

"But Robyn, you are so close to delivery time. You need to be careful."

"The baby is fine," She felt her stomach and put his hand on it so he could feel it too.

"I love you so much and I do not want anything to happen to you. You need to get well, Papa." She smiled and started to walk away.

"I think you should stay because I don't want anything to happen to you. Robyn I love you so much and I don't think I could live if anything happens to you."

"Hey buddy you are stuck with me and you need to get that through your head."

"Robyn please don't go." He stared at the ceiling wishing that Alex or Emily would surprise them and go with her. As she was preparing for the trip, Mark followed her down the stairs still begging her to stay; the doorbell rang and Robyn opened the door and there stood Alex and Emily smiling mischievously. "G'day mate." Alex said in a mock Australian accent.

"I was just thinking about you," Mark said. He was sure they heard him.

"We wanted to surprise you and if you don't mind we would like to go with you." Alex explained. "I have some business to check on with Richard so we can all go together."

"Oh, you two!" Robyn knew that it would do no good to argue with them. "I know when you two make up your minds there is no changing them!"

Alex grinned and pointed to Emily, "It's her fault."

As they were loading the car, Alex looked back at Mark and winked. "Don't worry we will take good care of her."

Mark sat back in his chair and shook his head. "How does she do that?" He was glad that she did. It seemed Emily always knew what he was thinking. But he had seen it not just with him but others too. He looked up and said, "Thank you God for giving Emily that gift. I don't know what I would do without my Robyn. Please protect her and my friends."

Upon arrival they checked in a hotel and Emily insisted on Robyn resting for a few minutes before going to the office. While she attended to her business, Emily went shopping and Alex went to see Richard. When everyone's business was completed they met at their favorite restaurant for lunch. After lunch Robyn went to rest and Alex and Emily took a water taxi and visited the bay. Later, strolling along the streets Alex walked a little taller holding Emily's hand. He wanted the whole world to know how lucky he was to have her. Emily always felt that heads turned because of Alex. He was tall, well-built, very muscular and handsome. Alex thought heads turned because of his beautiful wife. Neither realized that it was their obvious happiness that everyone noticed first.

Emily was exhausted as they joined Robyn for supper. Robyn looked very tired so after they ate Alex insisted on helping Robyn to her room. The next morning Alex told Robyn that he wanted to stay and take care of the rest of her business. Emily convinced her that she should agree. Robyn decided she did need to go home, so she told them she would listen to their suggestions. "I hate to spoil your fun, but I don't think business and this baby are a good mix."

"Not to worry! I came prepared to stay just in case this proved to be too much for you."

She hugged them both, "I love you two so much."

For once Emily was glad for her premonitions. Alex took them to the airport and pulled Emily aside, "Take care of her; she looks very bad." Emily had noticed and tried to assure Alex that it was just because she was tired.

Once they were home they found Mark feeling better. However, he was shocked by Robyn's appearance. So Emily cooked supper and was getting ready to leave and Mark and Robyn begged her to stay.

She called Kate and told her that she would be staying overnight. After supper Robyn went straight to bed and both Mark and Emily noticed that she had not eaten very much.

"Mark I think you should stay close for the next few days."

Knowing from the dream incident at Christmas, he knew that Emily sensed things. "Emily did she say anything? Did you sense anything?" He had not quite come to terms of the discovery of her dreams and how they tied in to her gift. "Please, tell me if you know."

"Of course I don't know anything. Don't be silly about that. She just needs you to be close. This trip took more energy than she really had." The whole subject made her uncomfortable, because at times she didn't understand this gift and at times she didn't want it either. "Just realize that she needs you close until she regains her strength."

After talking a bit, Robyn read some scriptures and prayed with Mark. Mark went up to bed with Robyn who was sleeping soundly. Emily went to sleep as soon as her head hit the pillow. She too was very tired. Shortly she began to dream again, *She was in a fog at first and images came and went through her dream. She saw Mark holding Robyn and he was crying. She was running toward them and then it was raining and thundering. She was once again standing at the ditch with Alex at the bottom lying beside his vehicle. She jumped into the ditch and grabbed Alex, shaking him she cried out, "Alex get up please. Wake up!" Someone was pulling her away it was Mark. "Come on Em. He's gone."* She awakened and was shocked to see Mark standing by her bed. Not sure at first if this was real…she rubbed her eyes. He asked, "Emily are you okay? You were calling out for Alex. Was it the dream again?"

The first part of her dream was clearer now and she said, "Mark hand me my robe. How's Robyn? Did I wake her too? Let's check on her now.'"

"I don't think you wakened her. I was downstairs reading, but she was fine when I checked on her. That's when I heard you call out."

He turned and looked at her, grabbing her by the shoulders, "You dreamed about her didn't you."

Not waiting for an answer they ran into Robyn's room. Robyn was in hard labor and Emily turned to Mark, "Call the doctor now. I don't think we have time to get to town."

She called Kate to come over and then everything was happening so fast. The doctor arrived and a storm had started, but Emily was numb to all of it. She worked endlessly doing what she was told to do. She remembered the doctor saying she and the baby were in trouble, but she was efficiently trying to comfort Robyn. Exhaustion was creeping up on her fast and Mark turned to see her growing pale. Not wanting to leave Robyn's side, he called to Kate and pointed to Emily.

Kate took Emily's hand and said, "You need some rest or at least let me get you some tea."

Emily allowed herself to be led away from the room. "Mark call me if anything happens. I am going to pray and rest."

"Emily I have been praying for God to spare her. Please pray too."

"I will." She turned and then turned back. She was going to add that God always knows what is best, but he had buried his head in the pillow beside Robyn's head and was praying, so she left. Not sure how much time had really passed she rested and sipped her tea. She prayed fervently for Robyn and Mark and the baby. Suddenly she heard Robyn cry out and she rushed to her side only to find that the baby had been born dead. The doctor said they couldn't move them to a hospital because of the storm and no helicopter could get there. He worked diligently with Robyn. He encouraged Mark to say his good-byes. "I have done all I can do." He turned and left Mark in the room while he went to clean up. Mark's eyes were full of tears and Robyn reached up to wipe them away, "Did you see him? Name him Mark Alex and bury us together."

Mark could barely speak "No baby, don't say that. I can't bear losing you."

"Sh! Now I will be the official heavenly greeter for our family. God is waiting for me. Little Mark is already there." They allowed the children to come in and say good-bye and then Kate finally got them all back to bed. Robyn was sinking fast from the loss of so much blood.

Looking at the pain on Mark's face was hard for her, "Mark the kids only have you now. Take good care of them and keep them in church. No matter what, you are their guide. I love you and will see you again.

I have to go now." Mark leaned over and kissed her as she took her last breath. He wished he could breathe life back in her body. He turned and wrapped the baby that Emily had washed and clothed, in a blanket that Emily had helped Robyn make. Kate and Emily had cleaned up before the children were brought in. He placed the baby beside his wife and very tenderly covered them both. He stood up but then fell to his knees and buried his face in the covers and cried uncontrollably. "Why? God please help me understand." At first he looked angrily toward heaven but Robyn's last request came into his mind and his anger left as quickly as it came. Placing his head beside Robyn's with his breaking heart he placed his hand on her face and as he felt the coldness set in, "Good-bye my darling." He kissed her and the baby and stood just staring down at them.

Emily checked on the children and they were sleeping. Hank was up and at his desk when she entered the room. He turned to her as she crossed the room to where he was, "Emily what are we going to do now?"

"Just be there for your Dad and the others. They all will need you to be strong now more than ever. You will have to grow up a bit faster. God will help you. I see you are reading His Word." She turned to a scripture in the Bible and told him that it always gave her comfort.

After leaving his room, she felt exhausted and her faith was being tested. She wished Alex was there as she went through the motions of helping Mark with the arrangements. She was sitting at the table with her head on her arms, "Oh Alex, I wish you were here. I need you. Be careful but get home soon." She felt a hand on her shoulder and turned to see Mark standing there. On his face was all the pain and heartbreak of losing his wife and baby, "Oh Mark I am so sorry." He reached out for her as she stood up and he was sobbing so hard and leaning on her so much that Emily was finding it hard to stand. They were standing there crying and holding each other, when Alex walked in. At first he thought only the baby had died, but then he saw Mark so completely falling apart. Then he heard Mark say, "Emily thanks for being here, I don't think I could have done this alone. How am I ever going to live without her?" Alex almost sank to his knees as he saw the look of despair on Emily's face-something he had never seen. He reached out and put his arms around them both. "Mark we will always be here for you." Hank came in and walked over to Mark. Mark turned and they buried their faces in each other's shoulders. "Dad I will be here too."

Emily and Alex held each other and the strength of Alex presence helped although she was questioning God. Realizing that her faith had been tested as never before and she needed extra strength so she prayed for God to help.

Alex was the first to regain his composure. Wiping tears from his eyes he said, "We need to be strong for the kids. They will be up soon." He put his hand on Mark's shoulder, "I have no words, man. Just know that I love you and I will be here for you."

Mark took Alex's hand and said, "I know Alex you don't have to say anything the fact that you and Emily are here says it all. I love you both."

Mark sat down and just stared at his hands. "I don't know what to do."

"Maybe you should go take a shower. We called the minister and he will be here soon." Kate had entered the room and took control of the situation. "Emily you should do the same. Alex, would you help me in the kitchen?"

After Mark cleaned up he came down to the kitchen. How Kate had cleaned up things was amazing and now she and Alex were cooking breakfast.

The minister came and talked to everyone first and then to Mark alone. "Mark, I do know what you are going through. Two years ago I lost my wife and daughter. Right now is the hardest time, first you grieve, and then you will become angry with God. Just don't stay there, because you will find that He is the one stable and sure thing you have. You may feel that He let you down, but I assure you that He didn't. He knows all and He will be there." They prayed and Mark seemed to be a bit stronger. "Mark you both have been good and faithful Christians and we know that we will see her again. I would love to speak on the love of God and His wisdom at the funeral if that's okay?"

"That will be fine and I really think she would like that. She always said God is wise and He is in control." They stood up and shook hands, "Thank you Pastor Sweeny for coming out so early. We...the children and I appreciate it. I would like Alex and Emily to come back in with us and we can all pray together before you go."

The funeral was beautiful and the message was full of God's love. They knew that even in death and loss God was there. Later the doctor told them that Robyn had cancer and had she or the baby lived they would have gone through a great deal of suffering. God did know what was best and of course death is never easy to accept. First you want to blame someone; you know that God isn't the one at fault, so you search for anyone else to be the reason. Focusing on doctors or other family members never brings anything but more pain. Then there are the "what ifs" that fill the mind. What if I had done this or that never brings help, but brings only sadness and despair. Emily was busy searching her mind for answers so she could reestablish her once unwavering faith. She was putting on a good front for everyone, but she in all reality was feeling very unsure and weak. Mark leaned heavily on Alex and her for help and assurance. They had stayed close. Robyn's mom came to help with the children and Hank was also a big help.

After the funeral was over in the car on the way home, Mark had looked at them and said, "Life goes on and I promised her I would be a good leader to our children." He bowed his head and the tears rolled down his face. He stared out the window and watched the scenery go by; he didn't want to feel anything.

Once they were alone, Alex reached down and touched Emily's face; he felt guilty that he was glad he still had her. "Honey...I could not have made it through what Mark has gone through. It would have totally destroyed me. You are my life and without you there's no point..." He shrugged his shoulders not being good with expressing deep feelings. Emily went up to him and leaned against his chest, while she gently cried.

Then suddenly it came to her. She looked up at him and there it was he saw the old Emily, "Alex, Robyn would not have been able to bury Mark either."

Upstairs in his room Mark stood in the center of the room. First he felt anger, pain, and fear, and then sadness overwhelmed him. He paced the floor trying to understand. But he knew in this situation there would never be understanding. The only place that made sense to him was with God. He knelt on his knees and with his face on the floor he begin praying with all his heart, *"I need you heavenly Father. I can't do this alone. Please help me God."* Suddenly almost as if an invisible hand had lifted him to his feet, he stood up. It was as if God was speaking directly to him saying *"I am here. Lean on me."* Emily was right. She had told him to lean on God. He'd never really had to lean before. He knew that from now on he would be leaning all the time, because he had never felt such peace. Now he was willing to put God in control of his life. He knelt once more and prayed, *"God, please give me strength that I need to raise good Christian children. Help me to follow your will for my life. Thank you for giving me Robyn at least for a little while. Take care of her and little Mark. I may not understand losing her, but I thank you for sparing her the pain that she would have suffered. And thank you for sending the Daniels to us."*

He got up and started toward the door and paused, *"One more thing, help my hurt to mend and don't let it consume me."*

Turning to leave he was surprised to see Hank standing there. "Dad, don't forget that I am here for you." Mark hugged his son and together they walked down stairs. He felt calm as he joined his friends.

Alex and Emily were surprised to see him coming down the stairs and she searched his face, "Mark we can handle things if you want to rest."

"Thanks Em, but I learned something from you. God helps if I lean on Him. You remember when you told me that. Well feelings were rushing at me and I wasn't sure if I wanted to feel anything. First I wanted to be angry at God and I couldn't understand why He took her. Instead I found myself on my knees begging God to help me." He paused looking away to gain composure, "He really listens and He cares. He helped me have peace in my heart. I still don't understand, but I know that no matter what God is right here beside me loving me and guiding me. All I have to do is trust Him. When I prayed I found my son standing there and that too gave me strength."

Emily smiled and said, "Come to the kitchen; we can have tea and sit a while."

They went had tea and talked about Robyn. They remembered the good times and thanked God for them. Mark said with a quiver in his voice, "I even thanked God for not letting her suffer." He looked away but when he turned toward them he had tears on his face. Emily went over to him and put her arms around his head. He leaned into her stomach and cried softly. Alex and Hank came over and put their arms around them and for a time they all grieved. Although he was dealing with it he was still in pain of loss. They stayed with him until nightfall.

On the way home she felt all of the pain and anguish of the last few days come rushing in. She remembered how he had fallen apart when Robyn died and she felt every pain in her heart. *"God forgive me for my lapse in faith. Help me to always trust You even when it's hard to understand."* She quietly prayed and Alex reached out for her hand as he often did when they drove. Alex interrupted her thoughts, "How does anyone deal with a loss without God in their life?"

She stared at him amazed that somehow he knew that she had been feeling doubt, "You know I haven't exactly been relying on God these last few days. I even have had doubts.

"What? Not you." He had seen a difference in her these last few days, but figured it was just exhaustion for all she had been through. "Honey, you are always the first to see reason." He was perplexed and a bit scared of Emily losing her faith.

"I don't know why but this has just been so very hard and I think I failed God by questioning him so much."

"Sweetheart, you are very tired and plus you have never been this close to someone who died. She was more like a sister." She quietly looked out the window and rode in silence.

At home they sat down beside each other in the swing on the porch. Emily stared at the sky and said, "I have been bitter since Robyn died and I don't see the reasoning of any of this."

She sounded so angry that Alex winced at the thought of her changing because of this. It was his turn to be stronger in the faith. "Honey it is hard and she was like your sister. I lost Mom and Dad and

Brian. I remember that you were by my side through all of that and I will be there for you through this. It is hard but with God's help we can get to the other side of this storm."

Alex was praying to God to help him know how to help her. He hugged her and took her in his arms. She snuggled close and held on to him as if she would never let go.

"Em we need to pray right now and they knelt and prayed. They asked God to guide them and help them. Alex in a strong voice prayed that God would give them peace. "Thanks Alex, I have needed that." Emily knew that she had to leave the burden with God and not be tempted to pick it back up. It was God who had the strength to carry it.

She kissed Alex and held him close. Realizing it was his arms that she had longed to have around her. They went upstairs and checked on the children. Kate had already put them to bed but Alex noticed Leigha's light was still on, "Hey girl, what are you still doing awake?" He asked as he entered her room.

"Dad, Hank is so upset and I don't know what to say or do to help him."

"Sugar, the only thing I know that will help is prayer. Just ask God for the wisdom to know what to do. It is something we all have to learn."

"This is so hard. I don't understand why."

"We may never know why, but it is a time for us to look more to God and trust Him to lead us. God doesn't make mistakes, not even in this sadness."

"Dad would you pray with me?"

They prayed and then he tucked her in and said, "I know you are too big to be tucked in, but let me enjoy it while I can." He kissed her and smiled down at his pretty daughter.

Closing her door he went into his room and Emily was just climbing into bed, "Is Leigha okay?"

"She wanted to pray with me. It seems that she cares more for Hank than she has let on. She was worried about him." He smiled at Emily and continued, "Our little girl is growing up."

"At least she found a good one." They agreed and settled down for the evening. "You know I think Mark is going to be okay." Alex nodded in agreement. Emily trembled at the thought of ever losing Alex. She refused to think about it. Once again they fell asleep in each other's arms.

Mark and the kids were often at their house and many nights they slept over. The kids loved it because they had family. Robyn's mom had only been able to stay for a few days and now the house was lonelier to Mark. He had told them that nights were the hardest and several times he had awakened and reached out for her. Emily and Alex both were thankful that they had each other. Mark's pain would come through his resolve sometimes and he knew that his friends could see. He prayed harder at those times and always came through with added strength.

Mark and Alex grew closer and the two of them were always together. The two families had blended into one big family. His children had turned to Emily when they needed a mom. She didn't seem to mind. Mark thanked God over and over for the Daniels and what they had come to mean to them. Nights were hard for Mark and often he went to sleep hugging Robyn's pillow. At times the emptiness he felt was unbearable. He found that when he watched Alex and Emily together he missed Robyn even more. He turned more and more to God and found himself growing closer and wiser as he studied the Word. He was hoping that someday he might grow strong enough to help someone else get through their pain.

The year passed fast and they all had grown stronger in the Lord and learned to cope with the loss of Robyn. It had been four years since the Daniels had come into their lives. He went to the kitchen and asked his cook to make a cake with Happy Anniversary on it. She looked at him as if he was losing it. Then he explained that it was four years ago when he met the Daniels. He said make extra because they will be coming later. He left and drove over to the Daniel's house. "I am going to make it. Thank you God,"

When he told them it had been four years they marveled, because it felt like they had always known each other. They all sat on the porch watching the children. Hank and Leigha were always with the horses, but it was obvious that they were closer than ever. Edward, Nancy and Erika sat in a huddle quietly talking. Ariel and the younger boys, Wesley and Lois, were playing in the tree house as usual.

The day had been enjoyable and Emily was the first to get up and gather everyone's glasses and then went to the kitchen. She had not talked much and Mark was alarmed. "Alex what is wrong with Emily. She barely talks any more. She is so pale and thin; is she okay?"

Alex paused for a moment and Mark was afraid he had intruded on something private. He started to apologize, but Alex began, "Well we have been sort of doing without sleep lately." Alex was speaking very quietly. An apparent burden was weighing him down and he struggled to talk. Mark was going to try to change the subject knowing his friend was not good sharing his feelings, but Alex continued, "Mark I would like to talk to you, but not here. I can come over tomorrow when Emily takes the kids, yours too, into town for an all-day outing. We can talk then."

"I don't want to pry into your business."

"You aren't prying and man if you don't know this by now I look at you as a brother,"

The next day Emily went by and picked up Mark's kids and Alex stayed with Mark. After they had left, Mark and Alex saddled a couple of horses and went for a ride. Down by the lake they dismounted. Walking over to a bench that Mark had made for Robyn they sat down. Alex began haltingly, "Mark, I hope this doesn't upset you and that's why I hesitated to tell you. You might think it is crazy, but well I will try to explain."

"Alex, I am fine and God has strengthened me. So if I can help you I am here."

"Robyn's death has hit Emily harder than she lets on. You see she has dreams and has always had them. I have known about it all of her life. Well she dreamed about Robyn's death the night it happened." Alex got up and threw a rock in the lake. Turning to Mark he said, "She dreamed it all, and now she feels guilty that she wasn't able to see it in time to help. This wasn't the first time she has had a dream about things. It has happened in the past too."

Mark looked at his friend not really understanding about the dreams, "Alex, doesn't she realize that there was not one thing that she could have done. It was God's will and I know that beyond a shadow of a doubt. Would it help if I talked to her?"

Mark was standing in front of Alex and realized there was more. He had just began to know about her dreams and really wasn't sure he really understood them. "There's more I can see it in your face. Let it go."

"She says she doesn't want to sleep and dream. Worse than that she hasn't read her Bible in days and her mornings with God are gone. Those things always kept her grounded. She says she doesn't want to see the sunrise anymore. I can't help her. I feel so useless and helpless. She is holding everything inside and basically…she's shut me out." Alex looked into the distance and Mark could feel his worry.

"Alex I can talk to her if you think it will help."

"I don't know, but I have to do something."

"Mark there is one more thing…she has dreams about my death, too." Alex looked at his friend and said, "I know this is all hard to understand, but you see she dreamed about my Mom's death and my Dad's, but when my brother died she was hit hardest. Then after we came here she started dreaming about my death. At first it came in bits and pieces, she wasn't sure what the entire meaning was, but now it is full blown and she sees it all."

"So, she tells you about them."

"We always share everything. No secrets, but lately I feel shut out of that part of her life. I think I could deal with things if she would just talk to me."

"Alex her communication with you apparently comes from her lack of communion with God too. Let's pray about it now."

Mark and Alex knelt right there and prayed. "God will help us do the right thing."

When they arrived back at Mark's, they found Emily in the kitchen washing dishes. Emily had told the cook that she could leave and that she would clean up.

"Alex is out rounding up the kids. He paused and said to himself 'Lord help me.' Then he asked, "Emily can I talk to you for a moment?"

She wiped her hands and sat down at the table, looking puzzled, "Sure I am always here for you."

"I need to tell you something. You and Alex mean the world to me. You two have been an inspiration to me and my children. I am closer to God than I ever have been because of the influence that you both have been to me. Not only, did Robyn and I draw closer to God, but also as man and wife. We learned the importance of communication and it helped us grow closer as a couple. I don't know why God took her, but I do know that as Alex always says, God doesn't make mistakes. Emily we make the mistakes when we run from God or turn our backs on Him. I know that now. But you know that He is still there just waiting on us to come back. I know that all I had to do was give over to His will and He gave me peace." Mark looked at Emily and she was quietly staring back at him. He couldn't read her face so he wasn't sure what she was feeling. "The one thing I do know is that God has a purpose in everything He does."

Mark was standing in front of her. Looking at him she knew that he had grown strong in the Lord. She knew all these things and missed her closeness to God but she had faltered and turned from God. Tears began running down her checks and Mark was afraid he might have said too much. "Mark I shut God out. I miss Him but I can't pray. The words just won't come." She paused and then continued, not sure about telling him about her dreams. "I can't stand to face…" She put her hands over her face and cried softly. Mark understood Alex's feeling of helplessness. He wasn't sure what to do. "I can't stand seeing you like this. Please let me help." Then suddenly he realized that it wasn't Robyn's death but Alex's death in the dream that was upsetting her. "Your dreams are a problem. You dreamed about Robyn's death and from the few times we have talked I know you are dreaming about Alex too. That's why you are afraid to let go."

She looked at him and realized that Alex had told him about her dream. Looking into his eyes she could see only concern and understanding.

"Yes, I can't take dream any longer. If it is like the others I have dreamed it will come true and then I will lose the only man I have ever loved."

She looked up at Mark and knew that she should stop before she upset him knowing his loss was still there, but something in his eyes told her to continue, "He is the only man I have ever loved or ever will love." Shakily she continued, "I am losing control and I can't stop it. Help me Mark. I want this to end."

Alex was at the door listening as Emily held on to Mark's hand and begged him for help.

"Emily I feel my heart breaking when I think about Robyn, but I find strength in God because He was waiting for me to put my hand in His and I know He is missing you more than anything He wants you to come back to Him. Give in and give it to God. For the first time in my life I know where to find peace and help. I know that you know this, because I learned it from you and …just let go of all of this and let God take over."

Alex quietly entered the room and stood on the other side of her. They all knelt and prayed and when they got up, Alex picked her up and held her close. Mark felt that all the burdens had lifted. Alex looking at his friend gratefully said "We are going to make it."

As they drove away Mark felt he had finally been able to share his feelings and that he actually had helped. This had been a great anniversary. After putting the children to bed, he sat down and read in his Bible. He prayed, *"Lord, I know I will make it as long as You are with me. Help Emily and Alex come back to you. If it is possible let her have some time out from the dreams. If it is your will please put it off for at least another year."*

Mark didn't know for sure that God would answer that prayer, but he knew that God would give her the peace that they had asked Him to give. But as Alex and Emily soon found out that God did answer the prayer and the next year was a good year. Emily and Alex were happier than ever. Mark and the kids often stayed overnight with the Daniels. The kids were always happy about spending extra time with them. Alex and Mark spent many hours talking. Alex had confided in Mark and they often prayed together. Mark began having devotion times with his children. He learned how by following the example that Alex had set. Alex told Mark that Emily had gone back to having her quiet time with God. It had made all the difference in her spirit.

Alex told Mark that it was his talk with her that was the changing point. Mark however assured him that it was God who changed things and that God had used him to help. He felt sure that he would never have been able to speak to her without God's help. After all when he finally realized that the reason he had blocked God from his own life by not communicating with God on a daily basis. Once he had released his own will and given God first place in his life he had received a new peace and strength that only God could give.

God gave them all another year and they all had become even closer. Mark's house was being remodeled and they were staying with Alex and Emily while the building was being done. Mark awakened early several mornings and had watched as Emily passed by his door. She was once more enjoying spending her time with God and you could always see the peace on her face as she passed. But the day came when she walked by and she had a painful expression on her face and her hand was over her mouth as if she was holding back a cry. Mark grabbed his robe and went to the door. He saw Alex standing in the hallway watching her descend the stairs. Alex had a look of shock and distress on his face that worried Mark. He walked over to stand beside his friend, "Hey are you okay? What's up?"

Alex shrugging his shoulders trying to put his thoughts in words, "Man I just…she cried out in her sleep again. It has been so long since she did that, it woke me up. This time she was asking God to take her instead of me." He looked at Mark with tears in his eyes. "I lost it and grabbed her, shook her to wake her up. Instead of understanding or comforting her, I just kept shaking her and told her to stop being so selfish. She just stared at me with a painful expression. I have never yelled at her. I know that she never expected me to be so mean." Alex was trying to keep his composure, "I lost control. I told her that God knew who should go or not. Then I told her that she had no right to ask God to leave me without her." Alex looked at Mark who had listened to his friend without making a comment. "I could never live without her. You have been so courageous in the loss of Robyn. But I know I would just fall apart."

"Alex you should go to her." Mark said in a solemn tone of voice.

"Mark could you go talk to her and tell her I am sorry. You are better with words than I am."

"Alex, you know, I would walk through fire for you, but this time it is not my place. You and you alone need to go to her."

"But I hurt her. I have never done that…ever." Alex hung his head shamefully.

"All the more reason you should go to her now." Mark patted Alex's shoulder in encouragement.

Knowing that Mark was right he walked hesitatingly downstairs and went to Emily. As Mark watched him go, he realized that Alex and Emily had never had any serious arguments. He went back to his room and knelt in prayer for his friends. *"Lord, I guess I should have asked for more time. Please help them work through this again. Give them your help."*

While walking toward Emily, Alex prayed for help. *'Please give me the words, Lord.'* Not sure what to do or what to say, he said, "Emily, I am so sorry."

She ran to him and he put his arms around her. Comforting her as he usually did after the dreams. They held each other for a few minutes and at the same time they said "I love you." Then Alex continued, "I didn't mean to scare you, baby. Please forgive me for being mean. But, I know that God doesn't make mistakes. He knows what is to be done or if it is to be that way. You are the light of my life. All of the things we have experienced in these past few years, just hit me how much I need you. I could never live without you!" She buried her face in his chest and her soft cries were shaking her whole body. Alex just held her close and stroked her hair as his big heart was breaking.

Mark was outside the kitchen door listening to her sobbing. She had always been so strong but now all he could see was her small hands on Alex's back while he comforted her. He felt such empathy for his friends. Quietly crossing over to pour coffee for his friends, as Emily regained control, then she and Alex prayed for forgiveness and strength. Once they had finished Mark took them coffee and a blanket for Emily. The three sat watching the sunrise while sipping their coffee. Then Mark said, "You know when Robyn died I wanted so much to die too. Then all I had to do was pray "God help me" and when I let go of my need to be in control then He was there. No matter what may happen, I never want to be without His peace. We can be close to Him but not fully understand just how present He can be when we relinquish our desires and control to His care. Maybe your dreams have a way of coming true and I may not fully understand them. It is hard to see things that could happen. But, Emily you aren't letting God minister to you and help you. Even Daniel had a hard time accepting God's revelations to him. God sent an angel to help to sustain him while he showed Daniel the truths that God wanted him to see. You have someone to help you through everything, but you have to let Him be there for you. I truly believe, God will help you through these dreams..." Mark paused and then looked at them both, "Just let go and let Him."

"What do you mean help me through...? They have only brought me pain and a feeling of loss." She was beginning to see Mark's point of view. "But I..."

Mark interrupted her by reaching out to them, "He gives you strength in all things. God knows our weaknesses and what we need even sometimes before we even know we need Him. I truly needed to have stronger faith and then you and Alex became a part of my life and I saw a side of knowing God I had never known. I know that God sent you both to me before I even knew I needed you. I truly believe that you are the type of person, Emily that will always need to know things. There is something in you that will drive you to know. In its own way that helps you. This is God's gift to you."

"I don't think I have ever thought about it in that way, but why Alex?"

"God knows and you know that we often have to trust in Him. We have to let go of ourselves and remember that we make mistakes, but God doesn't. I think we limit God by not listening to what He is telling us."

"Can I stand knowing that I might lose Alex?" Emily looked up at this big man that she loved so much.

He was smiling down at her, "We don't need to limit God. Remember He wants to be all for us but if we limit Him by placing limitations on Him it says basically that we don't trust Him by saying because I don't want this and I won't let You help me. Give in sweetheart let Him have lead. He knows everything and His plans are always best; you have to keep reminding yourself that God is in control and most of all He doesn't make mistakes, we do." Alex continued, as he tenderly looked at his wife. "I believe that Robyn could not have dealt with losing Mark. God alone knows why things happen and He gave Mark the strength that was needed. We need to fill our lives with more scriptures and less of ourselves. We need to stop limiting God."

"Emily, make every day count. Maybe it won't happen at all, or maybe it is a learning tool. You have had these dreams for five years and it could happen way into the future. Whatever it is I think one thing God is telling you is make every moment the best moment you can make it. Good times are always easiest to remember." Mark reached out and touched her shoulder.

Emily felt stronger and prayed to herself, *'God please help me.'* A tear rolled down her cheek as they faced the new day. Mark saw it as it rolled down her face and he struggled to keep his own composure. She had always been so strong but at this moment she seemed fragile and vulnerable as she leaned against Alex's chest. She was quieter and more at peace. He had been so worried about Emily's state of mind that he had forgotten that if the dreams were true, he might be losing a brother. He felt weak but then just as the thought came into his mind God's spirit came to comfort him; he realized that fear comes from Satan and he relinquished his mind to God to help him. It seemed that His voice was speaking to him and saying, *'be strong for the days to come'.*

Today they had all learned from this whole situation. It would be an eventful day and they had so much to ponder. Alex went to the kitchen table and picked up Emily's Bible and motioned for everyone to go outside to the porch, after they were seated outside, he spoke, "I am not good with my own words but God is and from this we need to remember what God has given to us through His Word." He read from Psalm 25:4-5, *"Show me Your ways, O LORD; Teach me Your paths.⁵ Lead me in Your truth and teach me, For You are the God of my salvation; On You I wait all the day."* Let's begin with a new strength and resolve to wait upon the Lord and let Him guide our paths." The three friends stood beside each other together to face the new day. Each one silently asked God for His help. Whatever the future held they would face it together with God at their side. Alex drew his wife closer and felt his heart soar with love for her. Mark felt his love for his friends increase in strength as he realized he had manage to us the strength God had given him. It was a beautiful beginning of another year together.

CHAPTER
EIGHT

~

Once again Emily was sitting on the porch as the day began. She always marveled at the colors of God's world. Since she had turned things over to God, she spent more time in the Word and her quiet time. This was her refuge from the turmoil of the dreams. She still had them but now she resigned herself to just watch them unfold. It had been a year since that eventful day on this very porch when she had finally listened and returned to her faith. It had been six years since they first came here. Alex had taken to the new life as if he was born to it. He now handled most of the business in both Melbourne and Sydney. She loved it here and although she missed Robyn life was good. Business seemed to be Alex's forte and not only were they bringing in money but he had invested in Mark's production business. It was also soaring financially. He commented to her one day, "You know honey doing all this has filled an empty spot in my life. I was meant to do this. Really when I got my MBA I never dreamed I would be using it." Smiling, she thought Alex was happiest when he was 'wheeling and dealing'.

A noise behind her brought her back from her daydream. She turned to see Leigha standing there.

"Mom I know this is your special time, but I really need to talk to you while everyone else is still asleep."

"Come sit beside me. You can come to me anytime. I will always be here for you. Now sweetie, tell me what has you upset?"

"Well, you see…Hank is coming to ask Dad a question today." She hesitated and then continued, "Were you and Dad serious when you said that you didn't even want to discuss marriage with us until we were 21?"

"You know I believe we were just joking around but seriously not wanting you to make hasty decisions. Hank wasn't even in the picture when we were discussing it. You are still very young, and marriage is a big step with a whole new set of problems to overcome." Emily had seen them getting close but she really was surprised that they had become serious.

"We have prayed about it and we feel God is in it. Each prayer we prayed was answered with a deep feeling that this was meant to be. Do you know what I mean?"

"Yes I do and I am happy for you. Hank is a good young man." Emily hugged her daughter, but at the same time she asked herself if she was really ready for this step.

"Do you think Dad will understand how much Hank and I love each other?" Emily's reply was interrupted by Alex clearing his throat. She looked up at him and nervously grinned.

"I hear that this Hank wants to marry my daughter." He was pretending to be mad standing there with his hands on his hips.

"Oh Daddy," she saw through his act and went and hugged him. "Do you understand and will you say yes?"

"Of course I understand and I have seen it coming as Mark has too." He grinned and hugged his pretty daughter. "Oh Daddy I love you!" She turned and happily went upstairs.

"Had you really seen this coming?" Had she been so wrapped up in herself that she hadn't seen it? "I knew they were close, but I thought we had more time."

"I see them together more than you do. At first they were trying not to show their feelings, and then I saw it. You know the look. It reminded me of how I felt about you when I was trying to hide my feelings." Sitting down beside her, "I know that they are young, but I feel they are right for each other. They both have good heads on their shoulders. It makes me a bit nostalgic remembering when we first got together."

"It is nice, but well I have to get busy designing a wedding gown." She grinned got up and bent down and gave Alex a hug. Emily stopped and added, "Do you think she will want me to design it?"

"Probably so, after all you are a famous Hollywood designer." He teased.

"I guess you are going to be teasing everyone all day today. I know that mood and I feel sorry for Hank!"

He got up and walked over to her, "Can't help myself. I just feel very good about this." Putting his fingers under her chin, he raised her face toward him and kissed her. "We are getting old."

After breakfast, Mark and the kids drove up, and Hank and Mark started for the front door while the children ran toward the backyard to join the other children. Hank had a nervous look on his face as he entered the house. Mark was behind him with an amused look on his face. Hank looked at her and nervously asked, "Is Alex home?"

"Yes he is in the library just go on in."

Hank was quite a bit taller than Mark but at this moment he looked like a scared little boy. He looked back at Mark who was trying to look serious, "Are you coming?"

"No son this is something you have to do alone."

He went in and softly closed the door behind him. Mark was holding his hand over his mouth and Emily was trying to hold back a laugh. "Shall we go to the living room, Em?"

"No, come to the sewing room I have a design I have been working on for Leigha's dress."

"I guess that means you two accept my son as your soon to be son-in-law."

Inside the sewing room she said, "Of course we do." Then she and Mark joined in laughter.

"Did you see the expression on Hank's face?" He laughed.

Back in the library, Alex was seated in the big chair when Hank entered. "Sir I have a question I would like to ask you if you have the time."

"Of course Hank have a seat." Hank sat down nervously and just blurted it out,

"I would like to ask for Leigha's hand."

Alex loved to joke and he sat there with a serious expression, "Well, that's a lot to ask. I don't know for sure if Leigha would like giving up her hand." Hank looked like he would faint if someone yelled 'boo' so, after a pause Alex continued, "Are you sure you only want her hand?"

That is when Hank realized Alex was joking with him, "I really want to marry her sir."

"Of course you do." Alex grinned and held out his hand and as they shook hands Alex reached out and hugged him. "I can't think of anyone else I want for a son-in-law."

Mark looked around the sewing room and remembered that he and Robyn were going to make one when they remodeled. He hadn't included it in the remodel after she died. Emily sensing that he was remembering Robyn showed him the design for Leigha's dress. "Wow, this is great. Has she seen it? It is fantastic."

"I want to go in town and get some material and everything I need." Since Emily had made a name for herself with her designs the local shops were willing to get anything she needed.

While they were looking at the design Leigha came in and looked as nervous as Hank had looked. "When will I know what Dad is saying?"

"Well why don't you just ask him?" Alex standing behind her was laughing.

'Hank grabbed her and said "It's okay."

"After I figured out that he wanted to marry her. First he just wanted her hand, so I had to question if she wanted to give one up."

"Really Dad!"

Everyone laughed and they left the sewing room and went to the living room. Hank knelt on one knee and formally asked Leigha to marry him. He then put a ring on her finger. It was Robyn's ring and Mark looked proud. They all ate lunch and the kids went out to play. It was a wonderful day and the group always enjoyed being together. After dinner was finished Alex asked everyone to meet in the library. The children joined them and they all sat and talked. Alex read some scriptures about how a man left his family chose a wife and the two became one. They prayed and then Mark and the kids left. Alex and Emily put the children to bed. Leigha was sitting on her bed looking at her ring. "It is so beautiful. Do you think Robyn would be happy that I am wearing it?"

"Of course she would hon. I know Mark was proud. It showed on his face when Hank put it on your finger."

Over the next few weeks Emily was busy preparing for the wedding. The invitations were sent and arrangements made for her parents and family who would also come. Mom and Dad would be here one week before the wedding and stay one week after the wedding. Having her Mom would be great. She found herself missing Robyn knowing that they would have been enjoying this time together. The colors of the wedding were to be multi-pastels, pink, yellow, peach, mint green, robin's egg blue and lavender.

The groom's men would wear grey tuxedos with cummerbunds that match the dresses worn by the bridesmaids. Each girl would wear a certain pastel and the groom's man that walked her would have a matching cummerbund. Nancy-green, Ariel-yellow, Erika-lavender; Debra-blue, Brandi-pink, and Elizabeth-peach a friend from the states with whom Leigha had stayed in touch were to be her bridesmaids.

"Hey Mom Hank just called and said he rented six grey tuxedos for the wedding. I told him only five but he said you told him six. Why?"

"Well if you could have anyone from the states to be here who would you choose?" Emily smiled at the surprise she was to give her daughter. "Oh that's easy! Elizabeth. She told me that she couldn't come." Noticing the grin on her mother's face she broke into an excited laugh, "You didn't Mom," then pointing to the peach dress knowing that it was Elizabeth's favorite color, "You did!" Kissing her mom and turning excitedly she said "I love you Mom! I have to tell Hank." As Leigha ran out Emily thought about how truly blessed she and Alex were. Their oldest child was soon to be married and to an incredible Christian young man. Leigha getting married at 18, Nancy at 17 was graduating early from high school at the top of her class, Ariel only 15, but also at the top of her class were all three precious gifts from God. Ariel wanted to be a chef and at 15 knew her way around the kitchen and Kate always commented that she was as good in the kitchen as she was after all these years. Somehow Emily thought her daughter would make a good teacher. Smiling Emily prayed tor herself, *"God, I know that I let my faith falter in the past and I also know that You forgave me and brought me out of that depression. Let our loved ones be happy now at the beginning of their lives together. Give Mark strength to bear up without Robyn at this time. More than anything I ask you to be with Alex. Always protect him and keep him safe. Thank you Lord."*

Putting away all the sewing things and straightening the sewing room, Emily paused and realized that all her prayers lately had always included Alex, and asking God to keep him safe.

She was so very blessed and now in her late thirties, God had given her a baby. She put her hand on her stomach and smiled. She had not told Alex yet. Picking just the right time to tell him wasn't easy with all the wedding planning. What she wanted was that special moment that would be a wonderful memory.

She was cleaning and singing and Alex and Mark had entered and stood watching her because it seemed the old Emily was back. Alex snuck up behind her and grabbed her and swung her around. Giggling she laughed and said, "Put me down Tarzan!"

"Him Tarzan, you Jane?" Mark mocked them, "Give me a break."

Alex put her down and gave her a little kiss. Shrugged his shoulders and "What can I say? She brings out the beast in me."

"We are headed to town to pick up a few things. Do you want anything?" Mark grinned.

"Well of course I do." She went to her desk and pulled out a sheet of paper.

"Look Mark I bet it's a list already made." Alex grinned at Mark. Taking the paper and looking at it, he looked at her and then at Mark. "It's a prescription. What…? It is for prenatal vitamins." He turned pale and then reached out for her. "Are you? Does that mean?" He picked her up and gently kissed her. "How long?" Looking at her it was obvious that he was overwhelmed because he only spoke in short sentences.

"I found out last week and I have been waiting for the right time to tell you."

"Well now he will be insufferable all day!" Mark teased and patted Alex on the back. "You old son of a gun!" Turning to Emily her gave her a quick hug and said "Congratulations!

They told her to take it easy and like a couple of kids they left laughing and jokingly punching each other. Emily shook her head and knew this had been a good time to tell him. Looking around the room she was glad everything was ready. Her parents would be arriving soon and Mom would help her put the final touches on things. She was excellent at organizing and knowing just what needed doing. Every room was set for her guests and Emily was glad that she had plenty of rooms. Pam and Kate had readied the rooms on the third floor.

That afternoon she and Alex took a horseback ride to their favorite little spot that they loved to go. Alex and Mark had fixed this area up. It had a nice grassy area beside a creek, a large tree shaded the area. A large soft mossy area grew close to the tree by the creek. Alex had made a bench and placed it by the tree where they could sit. Often she brought a blanket so they could lounge on the soft grass beside the creek. It was their secret spot and only she and Alex knew it. Of course Mark knew because Alex had shown it to him when he needed help getting it fixed up before showing it to her. Other than the three of them no one else knew about this place. It was totally private and hidden even from prying eyes even if anyone happened to be close by. But with the size of their property, that would be rare. She and Alex often came here to be alone. They tied their horses by the creek and made their way to the grassy area. At first they just danced slowly swaying to music that only they could hear. Alex took a blanket from the saddlebags and spread it on the ground. They thoroughly enjoyed each other and the quiet of this time together. They made love right there in their own private area. Both full of love and renewed in spirit they returned home, gladly looking forward to the days to come.

That short interlude proved to be the haven in the midst of the storm. Whirlwinds of both preparation and anticipation filled the house. The colorful flowers in the garden were both vibrant and fragrant as everything was set up. Emily was so glad that her Mom had arrived early because she always had a take charge attitude and never seemed to lack the insight to know what needed to be done and how it needed to be accomplish. Watching her Mom working always made Emily feel proud of her efficiency under pressure.

The day of the wedding arrived with clear skies and beauty with all the flowers and decorations for the ceremony looking fresh and crisp. Soon the garden was full of the guest for the day. Everyone was quiet as the beautiful flute music summoned the beginning of the procession. Each girl entered carrying bouquets of pastel flowers that matched their dresses. As they entered a groom's man offered his arm and together they walked down the aisle. As they neared the front they separated with groom's men on one side and bride's maids on the other side.

Each of the wedding party entered in the following order-Brandi and Steve, Debra and Louis, Erika and Michael, Ariel and Wesley, Nancy and Edward and then Elizabeth and Mark. Leigha had asked Nancy to be her maid of honor, but when Nancy found out that Elizabeth was coming she insisted that Elizabeth should be the maid of honor. Leigha told Nancy she was always her special maid of honor because of it. Mark was Hank's best man. As Emily was watching and thinking about each girl, the bridal music began and everyone stood and turned to watch as Leigha entered on Alex's arm. He looked so proud beside his lovely daughter. Her dress was form fitting with layers of lace accenting her form. It was beautiful and it featured her best areas. Curls piled on her head were accompanied by baby's breath, lace and pearls and bridal illusion cascaded down her back. She carried a multi-pastel bouquet. Hank's eyes were locked on her as hers were on him as she walked down the aisle.

Alex's tuxedo was matched to the other groom's men and his cummerbund matched Emily's light turquoise dress. At the front, Hank stood tall in a white tuxedo and white cummerbund, smiling as Leigha walked down the aisle toward him. Alex proudly relinquished his daughter to Hank. He kissed Leigha and placed her hand in Hanks and then took his seat beside Emily.

After the vows were said, Hank kissed his new bride and then they faced each other and sang a song to each other. Then the minister presented them to everyone as Mr. and Mrs. Hank Garrett.

The reception went without a hitch. Emily hugged her mom, "Mom I couldn't have done this without you. Thanks for being here."

"You did an excellent job on the dresses and cummerbunds'. I love you and it was wonderful. I am so proud of you."

After the guests left, Leigha and Hank left for their honeymoon. Emily, her mom along with Alex and Mark they went to the cottage on Mark's land where the couple would live to prepare the cottage for the arrival of the couple. Dad was busy with all the kids back the house.

When the week ended and her parents had to depart Emily was sad to see them go. Once again she asked them to come here to live. As always her Dad said that he was too young to retire.

As the summer progressed and all the events that take place in the Christmas season brought peace and joy. Emily had forgotten how pregnancy slowed the body down. She began to look forward to the winter months when things would settle down a little. Sitting on the porch she felt a sense of calm because she felt that God had answered her prayers and not only taken her dreams away but had also given her a child. Her thoughts of Alex brought him and his features to mind. He looked good in his work clothes and in his suit when he came home from business trips. Thinking of all the different things that Alex did and all the love that he had for her and the children always left her feeling full and happy. With closed eyes she sat lost in her thoughts. Alex had been watching her quietly. Slowly slipping over and positioning himself directly in front of her so that when she opened her eyes she would see only him. Emily opened her eyes and smiled up at him. It never mattered how long they were together he still felt unending love for her. Careful because of her condition he reached down and gathered her into his arms. No words were necessary between them. Love spoke for itself. They went to their room and made love and fell asleep in each other's arms. As she lay sleeping in his arms, he watched her sleeping quietly. His heart was so full and a tear rolled down his cheek. He looked toward the ceiling knowing the secret he must keep. He now understood why she always held back things that upset her, because she too never wanted to worry anyone else. That is how he felt right now, knowing how she knew that God had blessed her because He had taken the dreams and given her a baby and to her it meant that God would spare him. Now when he awakened after each dream of Emily standing and crying in the rain, he felt helpless. Scenes of her screaming and begging him to get up, let him know that if the scene was reversed and it was her there…swallowing hard a realization hit him again-if it was her there he knew he would have died anyway. Nothing in this world would ever make him be able to live without her by his side. He knew in order to hide this from Emily he needed to talk to someone and there was only one person who would understand. Mark would listen and understand so he determined to set aside a time to talk with him. He never once asked God to take the dream away, wanting it to be his dream and not hers. He drifted off to sleep and he was floating into the dream once more but this time he viewed the scene with a detachment he had not felt. Seeing the scene he turned and walked away leaving her there crying in the rain.

The next morning Emily slipped quietly out of bed; after her Bible and prayer time, she poured her coffee and went out to the porch where she found a chill in the air. She returned to get a blanket and was surprised to see Alex there. He smiled at her, "Morning honey." He smiled trying to alleviate her questioning look. "Mark and I have a long day planned. Even though the bed was so comfortable I knew I couldn't sleep all day.

He put his arms around her and felt her shivering, "Alex do you have to go now?"

"No I can wait. What's wrong?"

"Can you stay for breakfast and watch the sunrise with me?"

"Sure babe, I would love that." He patted her shoulder and they walked to the porch. He couldn't help wondering if she had dreamed the dream. He was convinced of just that when as he was ready to leave she said, "If it rains please just stay at Mark's. I will be fine."

"Sure but will I be fine with only Mark for company?" He saw the look on her determined face. "Yes mother I will obey." He kissed her and headed off.

Driving down the road he could see her face from the dream-crying in the rain. Suddenly he realized that he had no feeling of fear at the scene of his own dead body. Mostly he just felt sad but not fear. God was always with him and would never leave him.

Mark was coming out of the barn as Alex drove up. "Hey man I just knew I would catch you sleeping."

"I am a busy man. What's up?"

"I need to talk. You know I am not good with words and especially serious words."

"Serious words? I see come on in the kitchen. Let's have some coffee. Rosa, my housekeeper is upstairs and the kids are at school."

They entered the kitchen and Mark poured coffee into two green mugs and placed them on the table where Alex was sitting.   As they sat at the table in the kitchen Mark was alarmed that his friend looked so worried. "What's going on?"

It's Em's dream…"

"Oh no is she dreaming again. That can't be good for the baby."

"Not that I know…It's me I am dreaming it now."

Mark looked at Alex, "You, too?" Mark shook his head and continued, "Man, I haven't wanted to say anything, but I have been having them too. I just figured better me than her."

"That's how I felt too. I saw it all and I saw myself dead. Only I didn't feel afraid or any feelings a person might expect. Mainly I felt incredible sadness watching her crying. In the one last night, I just turned and walked away. It was like I didn't care. It really hit me hard."

Mark just exhaled loudly, "I dream about having to pull her away from the scene." Then lowering his head he spoke shakily, "Reality in the possibility of losing you man is breaking me. You have been a brother to me. How long she has dealt with this in her mind is unreal."

Mark continued, "I think God is telling us that we need to be prepared for anything. We need to rely on Him now more than ever. No matter what happens I am there for you."

"My last trip to town I talked with Richard about legal aspects and funeral arrangements. In the event that it happens, he is prepared. He doesn't know about the dreams, and he thinks I was just being overly cautious. I have also left instructions for Pastor Sweeny about all arrangements. I remember how hard it was on you when Robyn died and I don't want her to have to deal with any of it." Pausing to gain his composure, "Of you my dear brother, I have a very important request…" At this point his resolve broke as he sat back in his chair then he looked down at his hands as a tear dropped to his knuckle. He reached up and wiped his eyes and looked Mark in the eyes, "Mark will you help her and take care of her? She will need someone to be there." He wanted to say more and wanted Mark to fully understand what he was asking of him. This talk was taking him out of his comfort zone, but he needed Mark to understand.

Mark sat there staring at his friend, "You know it, man." Wanting to say more but there was a huge lump in his throat and he was fighting to control his emotions.

"I think she will be strong in her faith, but she will need a strong arm to lean on. She was so young when we married. I am all she has ever known." Alex paused and looked away then continued. "It's the baby, the kids and most of all her that hurts the most. I want to see my children grow up and I want to stay with her. But I really think, God is telling me that my time is up and it would be wrong to ask for more time. Like the man in the Bible that cried for more time and he got it, but because of it many evil things happened." Closing his eyes he saw the picture of Emily's face in his mind. He looked up at Mark once more and then he lost control and put his head down on his arms and softly cried. He thanked God for Mark because at this moment more than anything he needed to talk with him.

Mark bowed his head and silently prayed, *"God help me be strong and tell me what to say."* Then the words came, "When Robyn died she told me she was going to get our place in heaven ready… and she would be our official greeter when we got there." "That's beautiful Mark. She was great you know."

"Yeah she was and I miss her every day. But you know God doesn't make mistakes. Isn't that what you always tell me?"

Alex got up and crossed to the window as he looked out not really seeing anything . He was trying to gather his words so maybe he could ask Mark. He turned to face Mark, "I worry about Emily and how she will cope, but I feel I have done as much as I can. The main reason I came here was to talk to you, but most important-will you take care of her?" He stared at Mark but the words wouldn't come. Did he have a right to ask of his friend what he was thinking? Would Mark even want to be there for her?

"Alex I will be there for her. I promise you that I will always be there as long as she needs me." Mark bringing his cup to the sink and placed his hand on Alex's shoulder said, "I love you man. I am glad you feel that you can ask me to do something this important."

"I feel the same way and Mark I believe you will be there for her…" He stopped wondering if Mark really understood his whole meaning. "Do you know what I mean?"

Mark had the feeling Alex wanted to say more but couldn't go on. So he reassured him once more, "I do and I will."

Alex turned and started for the door, then stopped without looking back, quietly said, "Love her if you can." With that he left and walked out to go home.

Mark stood there and quietly to the closed screen door answered, "I will and…I can." He was shaken and quietly said, *I could never take your place but I will give her my heart if she wants it.*

Both men gained what they needed from the talk. Unsaid words and feelings between them were somehow clear anyway. Alex was standing by his truck when Mark went outside after wiping his own eyes, he went over to Alex and they shook hands then hugged. Their bond was strong. Alex had never opened up with anyone the way he did with Mark. They tried to put it behind them. Mark waved as Alex left. It was not storming and neither did it storm for a while.

The next few months the two families were always together and the bond between them deepened as they prepared for the new baby. The children went to the states where it was summer to spend time with their grandparents. Larry and Kate were accompanying them which they always did when the kids traveled. Mark's kids had gone to spend time with their grandmother accompanied by Rosa. Hearing a car Emily went to the door, Mark was there.

"Oh I thought you might be Alex or the doctor."

Mark noticing pain on her face, worriedly took her by the arm and led her to the chair in the hallway, "Are you okay?"

"I am in labor." She said taking a deep breath.

Sudden images of Robyn and the night she died entered his mind, but immediately God strengthened him, "You should be upstairs. Or do you want me to take you to the doctor?"

"I can't make it upstairs or to the doctor." A labor pain hit her full force and she fell back in the chair in pain. "I am glad you are here. I have never had a baby at home alone. Mark I'm scared."

"Have you called the doctor?"

"Yes, and Alex should be here soon. Becky and Pam are on their way."

When the pain subsided he picked her up and carried her up the stairs. She was incredibly light, "Did you gain any weight with this pregnancy?"

"That's terrible thing to ask a pregnant lady."

As he placed her carefully on the bed another pain hit her. "Ow. It hurts…" she held tight to his arm as the pain hit full force.

"Oh great, what do I do?" He was close to panic but realized he needed to be strong. Then he heard the front door open. He yelled out, "We are up here. Hurry!"

Alex was at the top of the stairs in seconds, "Is she okay? What's wrong?"

"She is in labor and the doctor is on his way. Emily called Kate's daughter and Becky; they will be here soon. Her pains are only a few minutes apart."

The doorbell rang and Mark went to answer it, but Becky was already there answering it. The doctor entered and Mark yelled down, "We are here and the pains are only a minute apart. When they arrived in the room, Alex was already delivering the baby. As Mark stood there he felt the pain of losing Robyn and his son. He was glued to the spot as he watched the scene unfold. The doctor came in and Becky arrived with water and towels. They cleaned the baby and wrapped it in a clean towel. The doctor turned to Alex and said it's a boy. He was totally taken aback as Becky handed him his son. He went to Emily and placed the baby beside her to feed. "Emily smiled and said, "Hello little Robin Alexander." Both men looked at each other. Mark reached down and patted the baby's head. "Robin?" Looking at them he said "Thank you." Then he turned and walked out. Tears rolled down his face as he descended the stairs. He went to the kitchen where Kate's daughter was preparing coffee. He crossed over and sat down at the table, He was shaken but glad everything was okay. Trying to think only of trivial things to keep his mind clear was hard.

"Here you go Mr. Mark. I poured you some coffee."

"Thank you." He took the cup gratefully and started to drink. Alex entered the kitchen and crossed over and put his hand on Mark's shoulder. "Thanks for being here. I know it was hard for you...You were here for her." Alex spoke, "I wish that you had not had to witness that but I am glad that you came in when you did."

Mark reassuring his friend, "I am okay Alex. Being here for you two is my reward." He really meant that and then he added, "Hey thanks for naming him Robin. It means a great deal to me."

"You brother, mean more to us than you will ever know." Alex smiled and tried to lighten the mood.

"Well I guess we mean a lot to each other." Mark picked up on Alex's need for relief.

They sat sipping coffee and talking. It dawned on Alex that he had just helped deliver his own baby. "I did it Mark. I have never done anything like that in my whole life. Mark I have a son finally."

Mark saw a worried look on his friend's face as Alex commented, "I wonder if God will let me stay for a while. All my life I hoped for a son, and even if it is just a little while. I thought I was ready any time He saw fit to take me." Alex shook his head, "A son..." Shaking his head he added, "I really want to see him grow up."

"Alex just choose to be happy; take each day as it comes and make each moment count. This baby is a gift and what you both need right now. Anyway we don't really know what the dreams mean or what God's time table is."

They were happily taking care of the baby enjoying each day. Mark was often there and loved playing with the baby. However, the happiness was cut short when at two weeks he became very ill. He was med-flighted to Melbourne. The doctor said it was his little heart. He wasn't strong, but the doctor said he fought, but his little body simply wore out. Alex and Emily wrapped in grief went home. They took the baby to their private spot and buried him there. Emily was very strong, but Alex was grieving. He watched her hurting, but realized she was at peace. One morning as they were watching the sun rise Alex said, "Em, God answered my prayer. I wanted a son even if it was for just a little while, but I sort of meant for me to be the one to go."

"I remember when we prayed that prayer years ago. It's funny how you remember things like that at times like this."

"Em, I wish you could have had him always." '

"Me, too. But you know a real good man told me one time, 'God doesn't make mistakes."

Alex took her in his arms and they were standing there crying and hugging when Mark came out on the porch. He reached out and put his arms around his friends and grieved with them. The girls back in the states were grieving too. Emily asked that they stay for now. She knew it would be better on them and when they came home they would all go out to the baby's grave to put flowers on it.

When the children returned the job of raising them kept them busy. Emily found the loss easier to bear. Sometimes she thought about Robyn being there to greet little Robin when he got there. Heaven was a bit dearer because she had a good friend and her baby and now her own baby there.

Emily had a job making new designs for another picture. Alex and Mark were frequently on business trips into Sydney and Melbourne. Alex was now in charge of most of the business and had more and more responsibilities. Mark had laughed one day and commented that Alex was a natural businessman. "Everything he does makes money."

Emily thanked God for all the blessings. He had given Alex the mind and understanding of things. They also had been generous with their money, following in her uncle's footsteps; they gave money to their church, supported missions, and donated to several of God's works. She had built her parents a very large home complete with servant's quarters and made sure that they had a good retirement whenever her Dad was ready to retire. She also built a very nice garage apartment; they could rent for extra income. Alex had set up a housing company to oversee its care and up keep. Her Dad would never leave Arkansas. The time passed and then it was time for Nancy, Edward, and Erika to graduate from high school. Her parents had flown in for a graduation party. After the party Edward took Alex aside and asked for Nancy's hand in marriage. Alex shook his hand and welcomed him to the family. Nancy and Edward told everyone at the party their plans to be married as soon as they finished college. Hank and Leigha were joking with them both about being double related.

Emily couldn't help noticing that her parents treated Mark's kids like their own grandchildren. In fact the kids called them Grandma and Grandpa. It was another fun family time as they all sat enjoying the party. Winter would be coming soon so her parents left to return to Arkansas. It was obvious they really didn't want to leave and begged them to let the kids come too, even Mark's kids. So when they left, it was empty nest time. Hank and Leigha decided, they too would go for a short trip with them before Hank had to start his new job. It was a good time and they thanked God for His blessings.

CHAPTER
NINE

~

Sipping her coffee she had just finished her scripture studies and prayer time, and now she was reminiscing about life. Another year had passed the kids were once again in the states to spend summer with her parents. Leigha and Hank had given birth to a healthy son, Jeremiah David a few months ago. Talk about three proud grandparents, she Alex and Mark simply doted on him. Mark and Alex were always talking about what they would build for him and teach him. Emily was content to hold him and rock him. She loved to sing to him while she rocked him. Now that he was older Hank and Leigha decided to take a trip to the states so Jeremiah could meet his great-grandparents.

Larry and Kate went along also; yesterday Alex had taken them in to catch their flight and would be home tonight. Emily decided to stay and finish her sketches. Last night had been a restless night, because she never slept well when Alex was gone. The crisp cold air forced her to stay inside this morning. So here, she sat at the kitchen table sipping her coffee staring out the window. After eating some toast and finishing her coffee, she got up and got dressed. Then she went to her sewing room to finish her work. Realizing that her lack of a good night's rest had taken a toll on her she decided to put the finishing touches on the sketches and then rest. After the sketches were finished she put them in a courier envelop. The director had marveled at her designs and said much the same thing that Mark had said. "She crawls in your head and looks around to see what you want. Mark had laughed and said, "I told you so." As usual it embarrassed her, but Alex was there to rescue her, "It's a gift." Everyone had laughed.

The sketches now in order were ready to take to the director for final approval. Now she could go to take a nap. Settling back on the lounge chair her eyes were getting heavy. As she slept she found herself drifting off into a peaceful dream world. Here she saw every aspect of her life with Alex in clear vivid colors-when they first met, when they got married, when each child was born, when each child accepted Christ-then this house, their new friends, and all the happiness flooded her whole mind and soul bringing her a much needed peace.

Awakening she found it was darker and thought "Have I slept all day?" She crossed over to her desk and turned on the lamp. "Well if I have that just means that Alex will be home soon."

Then she looked out the window and saw the reason for the darkness. Dark grey clouds covered the sky. In the distance she heard the roll of thunder and then lighting lit up the far away sky.

That old uneasy feeling entered her mind and sent shivers down her spine and she felt an icy chill overtake her body. "Alex, don't come home not now." She spoke to the darkened sky. Closing her eyes and trying to send him her thoughts, "Think Alex, think and stay put." The doorbell startled her thoughts so she looked out the window there Mark's truck sat. She hurried to answer. Mark was standing there and noticed the look of despair on her face, so he smiled to let her know he was there with good news, "Alex called me from town; your phone lines are down and now mine are too. He wanted me to tell you that he was going to wait out the storm before starting home." Mark saw the relief on her face and then continued, "After I hung up I picked up the phone to call you and my line was dead."

"Come in," she stepped aside realizing that she had been frozen in fear. Taking his coat and hat, then placing it on the coat rack she said, "It's cold and I am sorry you had to get out in this" giving him a knowing look, "...but I "am glad you did."

He grinned, "He knew you would worry." She was mentally rebuking herself for having thoughts of doom.

"Hey Mark do you have to go right now or are your kids home alone, do you want some tea?" It was evident that she was still rattled.

"Yes I can stay, I left my kids huddled in the barn, and I would like some tea." He teased.

Emily shoved him and said, "You have been around Alex too long." Then she hesitated, "Did you really leave your kids in the barn?"

He broke out in laughter, "You really think I would do that? Robyn's mom picked them up yesterday and took them to spend time with her until August."

"You are giving me a hard time just like Alex. Sometimes, I believe you two really are brothers!"

Emily brought him some tea and small sandwiches that she had made.

"When this storm is over and Alex is back we need to go for a trip together. We can go in to Melbourne when you finish your sketches."

"They are finished."

He smiled and said "Of course they are."

Alex was in town at the diner, watching the skies. He wasn't sure that Mark had been able to hear him. Thinking about Emily and how this storm would worry her he saw the lightning was still flashing in the distance, but the rain was not that bad. Not being sure that Mark got the message or even was able to get it to her, All he could think about was Emily would be alone and scared without him. He wanted to be at her side, so he looked at the sky, he thought, "I can make it. It isn't that bad right now." Reason had left him as he thought only of getting to her. The storm was headed away from town, but it was still headed toward his home. He left the safety of the diner and started for home. The further he drove the worse the storm became, but he knew it was too late to turn back, besides he was less than a half mile from home. Thinking about being home was in his mind when a flash of lightning struck in front of him. Startled he swerved and lost control of his car. He felt the car hit the side of the road and then began to turn over. As he glanced around he knew where he was and at that moment a crushing pain sent him into darkness.

The doorbell rang as she and Mark were eating their lunch. "I wonder who that could be?" Mark followed her to the door, and there was a man standing there in the rain, "We could use some help there has been an accident down the road about a half mile."

"Yes of course!" As Mark put on his coat and hat, Emily grabbed hers and a first aid kit from the closet. "You going too?" She nodded as they went out the door.

Once in the truck she looked over at Mark and said, "At least Alex is safe."

Mark looked at her then back at the road; the fact that it was storming in her dream just hit him. A strange feeling overtook him as they pulled up to the site. Both of them realized this was the dream location. Emily jumped out of the truck crying, "Oh no, Mark it is the place of my dream." As he reached her, she was standing there saying over and over, "Don't be Alex, don't be Alex."

Mark saw a look of sheer panic on her face and then he looked at the vehicle in the ditch and knew it was Alex. He felt as if his heart would fail as they walked to the ditch just as the men were placing a body on the side of the vehicle. Emily without pause jumped into the ditch and ran over to Alex. She had also recognized it, but momentarily Mark stood frozen to the spot. A realistic picture of the one he had seen in his dream appeared before his eyes. Then Emily's scream brought him back to reality. "Please God I beg you! Not Alex! Please not my Alex!" A man was holding a light on the scene and Emily reached out and touched his crumpled body and then his cheek. "Oh, Alex, why did you come in this storm? I thought you were safe. Why didn't you stay there?" Tears flowed down her cheeks; she was crying so hard her body was shaking, "Alex please wake up be here, don't leave me alone." Alex coughed and reached out for her, "Em, I thought I could make it home." He coughed once more, "The phones were out...I didn't want you to be alone. I wanted to be with you." He reached up and wiped the tears falling down her cheek, "Don't cry, baby I love you so much." She bent down to kiss him and then his eyes closed and she felt him take his last breath.

"No! Don't die. Please don't leave me." She was crying in his neck and holding on to him with her whole might. Begging with every breath for him not to die, she sobbed. Feeling weak, Mark felt himself going into shock, but the sobs snapped him to reality as he remembered his promise to Alex, he prayed out loud, "God I need your strength. Please help me help her."

Emily had no one else but him and at this moment he knew he had to lean heavily on God. He went over to where his best-friend was lying on the ground and reached out to Emily.

She felt a hand reach out and pull her away, "Come on Emily let them finish here. Let's go." Folding her into his arms while she cried uncontrollably, he spoke softly to her while the rain washed his on tears away. "Em I am here and I will take you home now. I promised Alex that I would always look after you." They watched as they loaded Alex into an ambulance. Mark spoke to the medics and gave them his card. With his arm around her, they went to the truck. She sat staring out of the window just silently sniffling.

Not really sure what to say he prayed, *"God help me help her. You knew that she would need me so give me your strength."* He fought to control his emotions as he dealt with his own sorrow of losing his wife and child and now his best friend. Emily had become very quiet and Mark was afraid she might be slipping into shock, "Emily I will help you as much as I can. Please lean on me."

Emily looked at Mark as if she had never seen him before. He had been there the whole time and he had not left her side. He reached over and pulled her over beside him, "Just lean on me; I will be here for you."

"Thanks Mark." Wiping her tears with the sleeve of her coat, she leaned on his shoulder and closed her eyes. The only thing in her mind was Alex dying in the rain. The scene was etched in her mind forever. She felt herself slipping away, but couldn't stop it.

Mark took care of all the details and seemed to know just what to do. He called the family and made the funeral arrangements. As she found out it was already planned by Alex and she knew that even in death he was taking care of her. She felt as though she wasn't real. Everything was moving in slow motion. Speaking was hard and so she said very little, only answering briefly when others talked to her. After the funeral her house was filled with people who came to pay their last respects. Her world was confused at this moment. Searching the crowd of people she couldn't find Alex. She thought Alex never leaves me by myself when we have company.

As if a hand had touched Mark's shoulder he turned to look at Emily. Her face was one of utter confusion as she looked around the room. She was very pale and as she searched the room, Mark heard an inner voice saying *"Go to her."* Fearing she was about to fall apart Mark went to her side. "Em, why don't you go upstairs and rest for a while? I will bring you some tea." He could feel her pain knew she was totally confused.

"Mark where is Alex? He should be here. I can't find him." She looked at him and suddenly realized what she had just said. She placed her hand over her mouth to stifle a cry. Then her emotions overtook her and then she fell lifeless in Mark's arms. He reacted immediately as everyone gasped. He carried her up the stairs and gently laid her on the bed. He reached out and took a throw blanket and covered her. He knelt beside her and smoothed her hair. Mrs. McLeod had followed them upstairs and was watching him worry over her. "Mark is she okay?'

"She thinks he is still alive, Mom." He and Robyn had been calling the McLeod's Mom and Dad for years. He wiped a tear from Emily's face and got up and crossed over to Mom.

She noticed the strained look on Mark's face and to assure him she said, "Mark, she will be fine. It will take some time for her, but I believe she will come around."

Knowing that Mark would understand, she patted his shoulder. "I will go down and ask the others to leave and say good bye. Will you stay until I get back?"

He stood beside the bed and then pulled up a chair and sat down. Overwhelmed with his own feelings of grief he put his head down in his arms as he sat beside her. "God please help her. Don't let her lose her grip on reality. Give her your strength and...me too. You know I promised Alex to take care of her. I will keep that promise no matter what."

Emily awakened and reached out and touched Mark's head. She had heard his prayer and said, "Thanks Mark. I will be okay."

He lifted his head to look at her and noticed how pale she was, "Are you sure you are okay?

"I just forgot why everyone was here. None of this feels real. It just made me realize that Alex is …" pausing to choke back a sob. "You understand I know."

"Yes I do and I will be here as long as you want me to be."

"Honey," her Mom entered with tea. "Are you okay?"

Mark put a pillow behind her head and Mom gave her a cup of tea. "I thanked everyone for coming and asked them to let you rest. They have all gone home now."

"Thanks Mom. I'll be alright. I am suddenly very tired."

"It will take time baby. Mark will help you with things." Mom smiled and went out of the room.

"Maybe I should go, too, so you can sleep." Although he really wanted to stay he was afraid that she wouldn't feel free to rest if he stayed.

"Mark will you and the boys put him beside little Robin in our favorite spot?"

"Of course we will now you need to sleep."

"Please stay until I go to sleep." She looked at him pleadingly.

"Okay, I will." Picking up Alex's Bible from the night stand he read her favorite scripture, which Alex had told him and marked it in his Bible, "I will lift up mine eyes unto the hills, from whence cometh my help. My help cometh from the Lord who made heaven and earth." As Emily drifted off to sleep he waited until she was breathing evenly and then placed the Bible back on the nightstand. He covered her and kissed her forehead. He stood there for a moment watching her sleep. He understood firsthand how hard this will be for her. Both of them had been there for him and now he had to find strength to be there for her.

Leaving the room he found Mom waiting there. He put his arm around her shoulder and as they walked down the stairs they both had a feeling that Emily would be okay.

Early the next morning Emily went down to have her quiet time and as she sat there staring out the window, Kate and Larry came in. She turned to them with tears in her eyes, "My Alex is gone." They came and hugged her and she felt comforted. They were more like family than just employees.

Now that the funeral was over and Alex was now buried beside little Robin, she thought that she had cried until she had no more tears, until it came time for her parents to go home. They asked her to come back with them,

"Mom I can't leave. I have sketches to be approved and I need to be here in case changes are necessary. Richard said that I have papers to sign. Alex took care of most of the things but I still have responsibilities. Besides I would go crazy without anything to do. Here I have work to keep me busy."

Her mother patted her hand and grinned. Her father said, "Just rely on God Emily and He will help you heal. There is one more request we have for you."

"What would that be, Dad?"

"Well we have this great big empty house that you and Alex built for us complete with servant's quarters, which by the way we don't have." Dad was smiling. "Basically we want the children to come back with us."

She knew that the girls would be better with them and so she agreed. "I will take a while to heal and Mom you know so much how I am and being alone to have time to think things through. This will give me time to do that. You both will help the kids adjust. I will get stronger and get on my feet. In August when our weather improves, I will come to see you."

"Baby just put your faith in God and rely on Him to see you through. It will take time." Dad put his arms around her and hugged her. When they left, Kate and Larry agreed to go with them and so Pam and Carl took them to the airport.

A month passed and she was home alone again. Since the weather was still cold she was stuck inside. Sleep would not come; her bed was empty and lonely. At night she would stand there staring at it like it was a strange place. When she closed her eyes she could see Alex's face and hear him say, "God doesn't make mistakes, people do." To this she found herself talking aloud, "I know Alex, but I am still alone."

Finding her bedroom too hard to face, she began sleeping on the chaise lounge chair in her sewing room. She only slept three hours at a time. Nights were long and lonelier that she ever knew. When your love is gone, everything changes. People think you should just go on, but unless they have lost the love of their life they don't know. The things people said to her were kind and meant in a loving way, but sometimes she just wanted to run away when people were talking. Even in a crowd, she would feel lonely, because at those times all she saw was happy couples. She and Alex were always together, so crowds always made her miss him more. "Will I ever stop feeling like this?" Sometimes she felt like she wasn't listening to God and she would spend more time in the word and praying. "Alex I miss you." She looked up at the sky.

Mark had been on a business trip and she found that she had become used to having him around. Tired of being cooped up she was restless and wanted to go outside. Carl had finished taking care of the livestock and things outside. The ladies had already gone home for the day. She felt isolated and lonely so she decided to go for a horseback ride. Dressing warmly she started for the barn, but decided to walk instead. A good walk always cleared her mind.

The air was nippy but not as cold as it had been. She walked until her legs became shaky and then she stopped. Looking around she found that she was in front of the ditch where Alex died. Maybe if she looked long enough she would find him there waiting for her. "I miss you so much, Alex." She just stood there staring at the ditch oblivious to anything else around her.

Somewhere behind her a truck pulled up and stopped, but she was unaware until a hand touched her shoulder. Then an arm went around her shoulders, "I thought I might find you here."

Mark was speaking quietly but his voice was shaky. "Sometimes it is hard to say goodbye to those we love. The memories of the love you had will always be a part of you. It stays with you no matter how long or how much time passes. This is what makes the goodbyes so hard to say, but at the same time it is the memories that get you through each day." He paused, "I miss him too. He was like a brother to me."

Emily looked at Mark and saw the pain that was there and watched as a tear rolled down his cheek. She had been so lost in her grief that she had failed to realize his grief was still fresh in his mind. He placed his hands on her shoulders and turned to look at her. "I know that I am not Alex and that we both have lost a big part of our lives." He paused and then continued, "I can't take his place but I want you to know that I will always be here for you. Please lean on me whenever you need someone. I will listen and understand. I promised Alex that I would be here for you." He was begging her to take his help. At this point he stood there in front of her holding her at arm's length, but remembering his promise to Alex… was it just because of the promise or was it because he wanted to be here? "Just let me be here for you when you need me."

Emily was crying and he reached out and drew her closer, "I need you now Mark."

They stood in front of the ditch just holding each other. As they stood there both were thinking of their losses and together they grieved until their tears were completely spent.

Mark began a soft prayer for guidance in their paths asking God for strength and wisdom as they faced the future. God knew that they both would need a friend and so he sent them each other.

When they turned to leave, Emily said, "Thanks Mark."

He smiled thinking of the revelation he had received of God's provision, "God provides for us if we let Him. Come on I will take you home."

They had both said goodbye as they left God lifted the dark burdens that had oppressed them in their grief. Once again she could hear God saying, "Come unto me and I will give you rest."

Mark stopped in front of the house and turned to her and asked, "Are you better?"

"Can you stay? I could use some company. I really don't want to be alone right now."

"What's for lunch?" He teased, "If I am staying I need food! I am starving."

The whole mood was better and sadness was removed from them as they laughed together.

"I can find something. What do you want?"

"I would really like some pickles and peanut butter."

"Yuk, you would feel funny if I served you that."

The weeks passed and they found themselves together often. When August came she and Mark, and the boys flew to the states to pick up the kids. When they arrived, her parents and everyone was waiting. Ariel, Wesley, and Louis were so happy to see each other. Nancy and Edward were getting ready to start college. Michael had come to see Erika. They all were sitting in their corner of the table talking, and reviewing college catalogs. Mom and Dad pulled Mark and Emily aside. "Let's go in my study." Dad said. Once in the study Mom closed the door. Dad began, "As you know both Edward and Michael have been accepted to the University of Arkansas with full scholarships. They will be staying with us here in the garage apartment. Erika and Nancy will be staying with us too in their own bedrooms here. They both also received scholarships, too. Another thing that we want to ask is if we can also keep Ariel, Louis, and Wesley too. I know that it will leave you both without children but they really want to stay. Since you are already planning to come home Christmas you can take them home then."

Mom added, "We really want them to stay and I already have their home school lessons that you gave me. I have enough to make it until Christmas. If they finish before then you could send me more."

"But Mom that is so much work on you and Dad." Emily looked worried.

"Yes I know they are good kids but they can take a lot out of you." Mark added.

Larry and Kate interrupted, "We will stay if you would like. We know we are your employees, Emily, but we really like it here."

"Of course and they can stay in the servant's quarters that we never use." Mom laughed.

"Are you sure? As far as you being just employees, you both have been more like family to me. You will still be paid and I will consider this "hazard pay." Emily laughed.

When the family came back together, Mark asked the boys if they wanted to stay and of course they did and Ariel said she too wanted to stay. Plans were made and they enjoyed the rest of the visit.

When they left Emily and Mark were sitting on the plane, he said, "We are without kids, again."

"I know I miss them already." Emily looked at Mark with a questioning look, "Do you realize that Ariel is my last child at home?"

"Wow out of my six children, Hank is married, Edward and Erika are in college, little Mark is in heaven, and I only have Wesley and Louis left." They sat in silence and both of them thought about their children. It wasn't going to be the same without them.

"It is going to be strange without Wesley and Louis rough housing and asking to come to your house to see Ariel."

"Ariel was always the quiet one, but she still made her presence known. She loved to cook. You know we still have Hank and Leigha and little Jeremiah. They can come over more often. We can spoil the baby as much as we like."

"I am looking forward to Christmas." Mark smiled at her.

The trip was long but once it was over they made their way home Mark was thinking, '*I need to go often to see Emily so she doesn't get bored or maybe so I want get bored.*' From the moment they arrived they worked hard on Emily's business. Emily soon found that she too had a knack for business. Mark told her it was because of her ability to know people. They were spending a great deal of time together and had grown dependent on each other's companionship.

Christmas came and Mark and Emily flew in to Arkansas. They enjoyed the Christmas family closeness. The children although they missed home were not ready to come home. So as long as Kate and Larry agreed to stay too, they were allowed to stay. Larry said that they definitely wanted to stay. "I guess Mom and Dad have made Arkies out of you two."

Emily laughed. So once again they returned to Australia alone.

Back at home they were busy again, but Emily finished her designs for a new picture and sent them by courier to the director. She busied herself around the place. Mark had gone on a two week business trip so she hadn't seen him for a while. He called often to keep in touch. It seemed that she really missed him. She knew she was getting too dependent on him.

Looking out on the day she knew that the air was crisp and cool as winter was getting closer now. The day was pretty with a very slight breeze. Emily decided that she would take a short horse ride, so she dressed warmly. She felt compelled to go to her and Alex's favorite place taking some flowers to put on Alex and little Robin's grave.

Once there she stayed for a while looking around and thinking about how she and Alex had always liked to come here. As she observed the beauty of the place even at this time of the year, she was soon lost in thought about everything that had happened in the last few years. She put her arms around herself and remembered how she and Alex had swayed to music that they alone could hear. There had been so many changes, so much sorrow and yet so much joy and things for which to be thankful. She looked around and said "It seems like a lifetime ago since I lost you Alex. I miss you so much." Her thoughts made her lose all sense of time.

A sharp blast of cold air brought her back from her thoughts. It was getting cooler so she got on her horse and started back. Carl and Pam would already be gone home by now. She wasn't sure how long she had been gone. As she made her way back home a cold misting rain began to fall. She thought, 'maybe it will stay a drizzle', but just as she said that the rain fell down it large drops. Wet and cold, she finally made it to the barn. Carefully she put the horse up and took care of his needs. Patting him she said, "Sorry old boy to get you all wet." After drying him she put his cold weather blanket on him. "You will be okay big fella."

Her whole body shivered from being cold and wet. She knew she needed to get inside and get warm. Leaving the barn as she reached to close the barn door a blast of wind caught it and pulled it from her grip. Emily found herself knocked to the ground. She got up and grabbed the door again and managed to push it shut as the wind fought with her to control it. She reached to grab the latch to secure the door and a sudden jerk of the wind caused it to crash into her head. Dizzily getting up, she found herself fighting against the wind and the blow to her head was hard and she fought to not lose control of things. Managing to secure the latch she leaned against the barn as a wave of nausea swept over her, "I have to get inside fast." Her body was now shaking uncontrollably. Standing there leaning against the barn a wave of nausea swept over her.

Gathering her strength she ran for the house feeling the knot on her head. 'Great job Emily! No one around for miles and you go knock yourself silly!" As she reached the back door she found it locked so she ran for the front door. As she rounded the front of the house the cold wind was still blowing and the rain was pelting her already soaked body. A feeling of weakness caused her to feel extremely tired and dizzy. As she started up the steps darkness overtook her and her tiny form fell to the ground. *Opening her eyes she was in a beautiful blue room. It was warm and there was a large window there. She walked over to look out and she was amazed when she saw Alex playing with two little boys. She opened a door to go and join him, but Robyn was standing in her way. "Emily you have to go back. Mark cannot make it without you. He has found his strength in God because of you. You can't leave him! He can't lose you too." She turned and walked over to Alex and the children. They all turned and smiled at Emily and waved as the door slowly closed.* Once more she slipped into darkness.

Mark made his way toward Emily's house. He had been calling her all day and not getting an answer; he hurried to her. He had a feeling that she needed him. He prayed as he drove, "God don't take her please. Let her be okay." It was so hard not to think the worse after all they had been through. He was trying to think positive thoughts, as he pulled up looking around. He saw no lights on in the house, but as he turned into the drive he saw her lying on the ground. He jumped from the truck and ran to her. Finding her cold to the touch he felt as if his heart was beating in his throat. He leaned down and felt her breathing, "Thank God she is alive." Gently gathering her up and went immediately inside. While he carried her he was speaking softly and tenderly, "Baby stay with me please." He placed her on a large chair in the living room. He took a blanket from the ottoman and wrapped it around her. "I am here

Emily and I will take care of you. I am never going to leave you again. Please God don't take her." He was on his knees beside her begging her to wake up. She wasn't responding and she was still so very cold.

He called Dr. Gordon. "Please this is Mark Garrett, I am with Emily Daniels and I need to talk to the doctor it's an emergency." He was almost in a panic as he told the one who answered the phone, "I just got here and she was lying on the ground in the rain. And she is so cold."

"Mark this is Sara you need to calm down. Bob is out of town and won't be back until tomorrow."

"Do I need to bring her there?"

"Mark I need you to be calm. Tell me if she is breathing and if it is a labored breath or is it even?"

"It's even."

"Now check her pulse is it strong or weak and are her eyes dilated?"

"Weak pulse and her eyes aren't dilated."

"Listen very carefully now because you aren't sure how long she was in the cold, you need to warm her but slowly as not to send her into shock. First examine her to see if she has any injuries and make sure she isn't bleeding anywhere that you can see." Mark put the phone on speaker and as she gave him instructions he performed them. Finding no blood anywhere he felt a knot on her head. Examining it he didn't see any blood, but it was large and blue. He relayed the information as he went. "Listen carefully, now you need to remove her wet clothes and get her as dry as possible. Cover her in a blanket and if you don't have a fire going you need to start one but don't leave her too long. Once she awakens giving her something warm to drink will be good. Right now you need to try to awaken her. Go ahead and call me if you need me. I can't send a chopper in this weather."

"So I shouldn't try to bring her in?"

"No it is too far and she needs immediate attention. You will need to give her body heat if you can't get her warmed. To do that you must take your clothes off and lay beside her. If you get her warmed and if she doesn't wake-up call me again."

"I need to do what?" He said out loud as he carried her upstairs and gently undressed her with trembling hands trying to be as discrete as possible. He dried her with the blanket he had wrapped around her. Then he turned the bed down and placed her lifeless body under the cover. Thinking how lost he would be without her. He lit the fire in the fireplace in the bedroom. Moving in a trance he found himself talking aloud repeating Sara's instructions. As he brushed her hair from her face he said, "I love you, sweetheart." Gulping as he realized what he just said. He doubted she had heard him and as he worked to make her warm he hoped that he could tell her soon. He ran down to the kitchen and made some tea, put it in a thermos then hurried back to her and felt her body to find it still cold, so remembering Sara's instructions, he disrobed and prayed for strength as he crawled into bed beside her. She was so cold it made him shiver. He wrapped his arms around her and pulled the covers around her head and all. Some time passed as he lay there beside her. He felt her body begin to warm and his heart began to calm. Sitting up slightly he felt the knot and examined it once more. It wasn't quite as blue and it had not gotten bigger. He thought that was a good sign, but if I could just get her to awaken. "What am I thinking? I'd be … and well," but she did need to wake up. He prayed for strength because only God could give him super control. He felt sleepy and put his arms around her and snuggled closer, then he drifted off to sleep, praying the whole time *"God please let her live."*

He awakened when he felt her moving in his arms. Pulling her close he started praying out loud, "Thank you God for sparing her." She looked at him extremely puzzled, "Oh thank God you are okay. You are okay!" Crying tears of joy he held her close he was smiling from relief. Emily was still a bit groggy, as she soon realized that she was naked beside him. Looking into his blue tear filled eyes she blushed. Mark remembered that they were naked jumped up although he still had on his underwear, he grabbed a blanket from the floor. He was trying to explain to her why, "I found you and you were cold the doctor's wife told me to warm you and I didn't want to lose you. Emily please understand, I wasn't taking advantage…I couldn't lose you!"

Emily could see the concern in his eyes, and she smiled at him; then she giggled partly in embarrassment partly in relief. He came over to her with the blanket wrapped around him. He sat down on the bed and teased her, "You would laugh at a man trying to save your life?"

She reached out for him and he took her in his arms and she said "Thank you Mark."

He got up and picked up his clothes and started for the bathroom, as he walked away, she said, "You have to admit it was pretty funny seeing you, in your underwear, fumbling for a blanket and trying to talk too."

He stopped laughing and went to her and looked in her eyes to check for concussion and then examined the knot on her head. "I thought I had lost you." He looked at her and hesitated then continued speaking, "I am going to take care of you no matter what. I will never be apart from you again. With God's help I will never let anything happen to you." Carefully and gently he examined the knot on her head, she winced in pain and he asked, "How did that happen?"

"The latch on the barn door hit me in the head." She was feeling amazed at him at that moment. Her feelings were at first confusing, but in his eyes she saw nothing but truth and love.

He felt so much love for her and did not know if he should tell her how he felt. His heart was so heavy with emotion, not lust, but real genuine love. Looking into her eyes he leaned forward and kissed her a slow gentle kiss that spoke for him all he felt. As he drew back to leave he said, "I love you, Emily." At this moment she believed that she too loved him; she only knew that she did not want this moment to end. She looked at him and then pulled him back to her and returned his kiss. This kiss was longer and deeper. Sensing the need for control Emily pulled back and sat staring at him. Tears ran down her face and she said, "Mark, I don't want this situation to get out of control."

Mark looked at her swallowing hard; he reached out and covered her when the blanket almost fell away from her shoulder. "I love you more than I can ever tell you." He looked at her and then shaking his head smiled and went to get dressed. Coming out of the bathroom he gave Emily a cup of tea from the thermos he had sat on the night stand. "Drink this and I am going down to make some soup. Stay warm," He added another blanket to the bed. "And I will be back." Once downstairs he started the soup. He knew the ladies had all gone on holiday so it was up to him to take care of her, but he called the doctor just to be sure. Sara told him that he was on his way.

Emily drank the warm tea and felt herself feeling stronger. She decided to clean up and slowly got up from the bed, put on her robe and headed to the bathroom. She washed herself and carefully brushed her hair. She was dressed and sipping the rest of the tea when Mark entered.

"Emily I want you to know that the situation here is not why I said I love you. I do love you but it is real and I need you to understand that...I love you the way a man loves a woman. It isn't just friendship love but real genuine heart felt love." He was praying inside *'Please love me back'* and he continued, "I hope that someday, you can love me that way too."

She was sitting up on the bed and as she lay back against the pillow looking at the ceiling she said, "God did you hear that? He said he loves me." Not really realizing she was talking out loud. Mark was standing there looking at her with a smile on his face. His heart was full of joy as he heard her say, "I love him too. It feels right and I know it is."

Suddenly, she realized she said that out loud, she motioned to him, "Hey you! Come over here."

"Yes mam!" He walked over and looked into her eyes, "I am so glad you are okay."

She smiled up at him, "This is right I feel it."

He nodded in agreement and sat down beside her watching her sip her tea. "I made some soup and will bring it up to you."

"No Mark I want to go down to the kitchen."

The doorbell rang and he turned and gave her an order, "You stay right here. Don't try to come down the stairs alone. I didn't go through all of this to have you fall down stairs and break something."

"Yes sir." She smiled.

The doctor was at the door and Mark was relieved to see him. "How is she this morning? I came as soon as I got home."

"She made it through the night. Everything seems fine, but she has a huge knot from the barn latch hitting her in the head."

"Hypothermia is serious by itself without a head injury on top of that. Sara gave me the details that you knew at the time. I take it you know more because you know the nature of the head injury, now."

Emily called down "I am ready to come down there now." She was at the top of the stairs looking down at them. "He won't let me come down alone."

Mark grinned sheepishly, "Couldn't have her falling down the stairs and breaking something."

Mark helped her down the stairs and into the living room lounge chair where the doctor examined her. "Sara told me everything to do. That's one great woman you have. She calmed me down and helped me know what to do."

"You look fine and no hint of a brain injury but you have a mild concussion. No horseback riding or strenuous exercise for a few days young lady. The knot on your head will be sore for a while. Let me know immediately if you have any nausea or dizziness."

"Thank you Dr. Gordon, and thank Sara too. I am not sure what would have happened if it had not been for her." Mark humbly admitted.

"I think without you as well things could have ended rather badly. I am glad you called first instead of trying to bring her in."

"I have some soup on if you would like some." Mark offered.

"Sara has something prepared for me at home, so I better go for now. Take care of her. She doesn't need to be alone for now and also the next few days."

"Oh yes I intend to always take care of her. She is going to have a shadow for a while."

Shaking hands they said their goodbyes. Mark turned to find Emily just staring at him. She went to the kitchen with him and they had their soup. They ate quietly as the events of this day were fresh in their minds. Both of them had professed their love for each other and neither of them really had thought about what comes next. Mark cleaned up when they finished and Emily was sitting at the table just looking out the window. "What can I do for you?"

"I would like to go to the library." After he got her settled on the couch he covered her with a blanket and started a fire in the fireplace. "Mark do you have to leave?" she asked.

"Doc said I have to stay."

"Is that the only reason?" Emily still felt that this was all a dream and she didn't want to wake up any time soon.

"Emily, I never want to leave you again." He crossed over to the couch and sat down beside her. He placed his arm around her and she snuggled into his arms and quietly they sat watching the flames of the fire as it warmed the room.

Over the next few days they were constantly together. Mark stayed in the guestroom while she was in recovery from her injuries. The day came when they both realized that he had to go home.

Mark had been joining her in her morning sunrise watch. They had also established Bible study and prayer times. Mark had become more knowledgeable in the Bible and it was evident to her that he was studying the Word.

One evening after supper, they sat in the kitchen sipping tea. Emily saw a serious look on Mark's face. "Is something wrong?"

Mark took a long look are her wondering how to speak his mind truthfully. At the same time Emily was again wondering if this had all been a dream and now it was ending. Then Mark stood up and came and stood in front of her. "Sweetheart do you have any idea how hard it was for me the night you were hurt not to say 'away with morals? Then when you said that you loved me too, I wanted to make love to you at that moment and I have wanted you more every day since." He knelt down in front of her, "Emily I want to marry you. I don't want to leave you every evening; instead I want to wake up in the morning with you beside me."

Emily looked at him as if this was the first time she really noticed his features. He was tall, but not as tall as Alex had been, he looked at her with his clear blue eyes however his dark hair and ruggedly handsome features were not the reason for her love. It was his heart and his love for her and also his love for God.

"Mark, are you sure?" She placed her hands on his face, as she looked deeply into his eyes. He pulled her to her feet and kissed her very passionately. Her body trembled at his touch and she wanted him too.

"I need to make love to you…to feel you in my arms, to become one with you." Feeling her trembling, "I won't do that until we are married.

I want God to bless us and He can't if we start out the wrong way. That's why I am begging you to be my wife, before I..."

"I love you too, and I agree that we need to start out pleasing God."

He held her at arm's length to so he could look into her eyes. "Think about it Em. I believe with all my heart that God wanted us together. I even know in my heart that Alex and Robyn want us to be together. Even your accident has led us to proclaim and find our love. I feel God's hand."

"Mark I do agree...and there is something I want to share with you." She looked at him with all the love she had inside and continued, "The night that I lost consciousness, I dreamed that I was in a beautiful blue room with a large window. I looked out the window and saw Alex playing with two little boys and I opened a door to run to him." As she paused Mark was thinking, 'she isn't ready to let go of Alex'. Then she continued, "Robyn blocked my way...she told me to go back and not to leave you. She told me that you couldn't lose me too."

He felt as if he would fall over so he stood up and just pulled her close. They were both crying and Emily was praying to herself 'Please God let this be love and not lust.'

Mark stood back and looked at her as if he had read her mind, "It isn't you know?"

"What?" Wondering if she had said her prayer out loud, she looked up at him.

"It is not you know? It isn't lust or the fact that we miss our loved ones. This is given to us from God above."

He knelt and pulled her down beside him and they prayed together. Once they arose from prayer they both knew beyond any doubt that this relationship was from God. "We my love will begin this marriage as three-You, me, and God." Mark spoke in an even tone.

"When?" She smiled up at him feeling peace with life.

"Now! Right now!" He laughed. She was smiling but looking around the room.

"No minister," shrugging her shoulders. "I guess we will have to wait until tomorrow."

"That means I need to go home, but I will be back early and you need to be ready."

"I will." They kissed and both were happy as Mark waved goodbye.

The next day came and they planned to get married and then tell everyone. In three weeks they would be going to get the kids and they wanted to be married before that. The older children would also be coming home for the summer months (winter here) but for them it was their summer break. They were looking forward to letting everyone know their love.

After finishing loading the car for their trip into Melbourne to get married, Mark was in the house and Emily was checking the front door when Leigha and Hank drove up. "Hey Mom."

"Where's Jeremiah?" Emily asked.

"He is with his great-grandmother. We have the day off and we wondered if you two would like to go on a picnic with us?"

She answered briefly not wanting to let on how happy she was feeling today, "No."

Mark came out to see what was keeping her, "Oh hello you two." He too was trying to sound very calm.

"Dad we wanted you and Emily to go on a picnic with us."

"Can't, not today."

Leigha almost sounding like a little child, "Well why not?" Hank was picking up on the situation and felt that something was going on. "Rosa said you got up early to come over here. So what's up, a business trip?" He asked.

Seeing the disappointment on their children's faces they knew they had to tell them.

"Business, well sort of," Mark continued, "We are getting married today." Emily came and stood beside him.

Leigha stomped her foot, hands on her hips, and both Emily and Mark thought it meant that it was not to be blessed by their kids. "Of all the nerve!" Leigha looked at Hank, "We go to all the trouble of trying to get them together and they go and do it by themselves."

Relieved they laughed and then asked Hank and Leigha to go with them. They followed Emily and Mark into town. They stopped at the church where the pastor was waiting. They were married and then the kids went home while Emily and Mark went to Melbourne for their honeymoon.

When they were settled in their room and alone, He turned to her and smiled. He walked over to his pretty wife, "May I?" He started to undress her tenderly and carefully, "I don't have to close my eyes this time."

Their love making was beautiful and as they lay there totally spent they both were so thankful to God for His gifts. She had completely yielded herself to her husband and felt as if this would be a great marriage. He thought about how she had blushed at first, and then he felt complete as he too felt this marriage was a blessing from God.

When they were back at home it was decided that Mark would come live here because Emily still had another year before she received her full inheritance and this house could house all their family. So that evening after the evening meal when Pam and the others had gone to their homes, they were alone. Mark quietly led her up to their bedroom. Once they had finished their love making, Mark brushed a tear from her eye, "What's wrong baby?"

"I am so happy and I know without a doubt that this is where I belong."

"You are the part of my life that was missing since Robyn died. No one will ever convince me that I ever belonged anywhere else."

They fell peacefully to sleep. The next morning as it was Emily's custom she awakened and put on her robe. She smiled down at Mark sleeping so soundly. Then she turned and went down to the kitchen. She put some coffee on to brew while she had her Bible time. Pam would arrive later, unlike Kate who had learned her ways and was always there when she got up. After she was finished with her prayer and her Bible time, she opened the curtain to watch the sunrise, because it was too cold to sit on the porch.

Back upstairs Mark rolled over and found her gone, and he jumped out of the bed grabbing his robe he ran down the stairs and entered the kitchen His heart felt like it would stop beating at any moment. "Oh what a relief, you are real. I thought I was dreaming and that ..."

Emily crossed over to him placing her finger over his lips, "I am here."

He reached out and pulled her close before smothering her with kisses. "I never want to be without you…Not ever."

She held up her hand pointed to her ring, and then took his hand and pointed to his ring.

"You are kind of stuck with me now." She grinned at him.

"Emily, make me a promise. When you get up will you always wake me?"

"Yes of course Mark. I am just used to getting up early."

"I know, but I didn't like waking to find an empty spot beside me. It is too…well you know."

He knew that she understood an empty bed, even though she had told him she usually slept on the lounge couch in the sewing room after Alex died. He remembered the mornings after Robyn died how empty he had felt. He knew he never wanted that feeling to return. Taking her hand he asked, "If it is okay, I would like to join you some mornings?"

"I would like that Mark. I want to share every part of my life with you."

"Will you tell me about your dream of Robyn and Alex again?" Mark asked.

She told him how Robyn had told her to come to him and then how they were happy and all waved bye to her just before she slipped into darkness. Then how she felt when she regained consciousness and found him there jumping up grabbing a blanket and talking a mile a minute. She teased him and they laughed. They went upstairs and got dressed before coming down for coffee. Pam was there making breakfast and smiled when they came in. Emily showed her ring and grinned.

She and Mark finished breakfast and went into the library to relax. Emily played a hymn on the piano and Mark started singing the words. They smiled at each other and both were happy to begin their new life together.

Mark sat down on the stool beside her and said, "You know Emily I think Robyn was right. I would have given up if I lost you." He held her close and stroked her hair. They had lost so much but receive so much too. Emily felt lucky, no not luck that left too much to chance. She knew they were blessed and that blessing came from God and God alone.

Mark wondered aloud, "I wonder what the future holds for us. We have to trust God's plans no matter what."

Emily grinned as she could almost hear Alex saying these words, "God doesn't make mistakes, only people make them."

CHAPTER
TEN

~

Life continues and new bonds are made and discovered as she sat contemplating all the changes she felt in her heart that she and Mark belonged together as part of God's plan. She entered into the business world and Emily and Mark were finding how admired Alex had become to the employees and coworkers. Alex's business abilities were office legend. They told her how easy it was to work with him. He not only knew how to lead but he had a knack for making money. To her own amazement Emily discovered that she too found the business world a comfortable place. Mark told her she also had the capability for making money just like Alex had done. When she first found out the extent of her assets and holdings she felt a deep overwhelming sense of wonder. Soon she would be the one in control of all this. Thankful that there were trusted employees around her made it easier to bear. Because of Richard she knew that she was in good hands. She never ceased to give God the glory and her thanks. Alex's short time there had increased the amount of assets by twenty percent.

Back at home all of the family was now together. The older children were home from college and the younger ones had returned from their grandparent's home. Hank, Leah and Jeremiah moved into Mark's house with Rosa as their housekeeper. Both Mark and Emily's families were now under one roof as one family.

She sat on the porch reminiscing about the things that had been, and all the things that were happening now. Mark came out to the porch and stood watching her; somehow he felt that she was thinking about everything they had experienced. He didn't know nor did he fully understand the bond between them, but he somehow could sense her feelings. It was like he now had her sixth sense. Moving over to where she was sitting, he sat down beside her. Then he placed his arm around her and they sat silently watching the sunrise above the horizon. Smiling as the sunlight brought out the beautiful bright colors of the day, he said, "I love this time and being able to be with you."

"Yes me too. It just all seems so right." With that statement Mark felt that she was comfortable with all the changes. She had a glimmer in her eye and started out pretending to be serious, but added, "Mark you know I love you, but sometimes you are a bit nuts!" She laughed and jumped up to run.

"Nuts am I?" He caught her and threw her over his shoulder and carried her into the house. Kate and Pam were in the kitchen and turned and began to laugh at them. "Ladies, I can't do anything with her. She keeps getting out of hand." Then he left the kitchen and started for the stairs.

"Let me down. All the blood is rushing to my head." She was yelling playfully and all the kids rushed to see what was happening.

"Hey Dad what's up?" Wesley concerned at first, but then saw Emily's smile so he grinned. Louis just stood there with his mouth wide open.

"Close your mouth, son. You're drawing flies." Mark teased. "I am just giving her a lift up the stairs. She is a grandma you know."

"Uh-um," Clearing her throat, "And Dad you're a grandpa." Erika reminded him.

"That's right I am." Putting Emily down, he feigned having a bad back, "Dearie help me to the bedroom."

"Make it on your own 'dearie' I am in pretty good shape for a 'grandma'. She shoved him. "I don't have a bad back."

"That's because I carry you most of the time." He laughed and swatted her bottom.

Edward and Nancy were shaking their heads, "I think they are getting senile."

"I think the high altitudes are getting to them." Ariel laughed.

"Maybe we need to fix them a room on the main floor." Nancy added.

"Good idea! I am not carrying anyone up those stairs." Edward exclaimed.

The children were all laughing and joking when Mark held up his hands to calm them.

"Everyone get dressed, the ladies have prepared a tasty breakfast for us. After we are finished we will be going on an extended family vacation. We will fly to Melbourne to complete some business and on to Sydney where we have to meet with some producers to show Emily's designs, after that, we are all going to Hawaii. Don't worry about packing it has all been done except your personal items, but I think you guys can handle that."

Emily never ceased to be amazed at Mark's spontaneity, "You planned all of this. Did you send my new designs in too?"

He grinned mischievously. I want this to be a vacation to remember. It is our family honeymoon."

When they were in Melbourne finishing up their business, the children were having fun shopping and seeing the sights. Emily found that she was partial to Melbourne but both cities were fun to visit. Once they were in Sydney at the design offices Emily was viewing their contracts. After receiving several requests from directors and producers for her designs, she had meticulously viewed each one and script. Several she had already refused because as she said the scripts were 'sick'. She refused anything that she felt was not pleasing to God. That is one part of this business with which she refused to be a part.

Mark was telling her, "If I ever get back into this business as a director, I might consider some acting or even writing."

"You are good at all of those things. I saw you act in a few of those tapes at home. I didn't finish the ones where they used all the foul language. It upset me to hear you say those words."

"You amaze me sometimes. The only thing I need is some good material to write about. I want something that is good not just hype like most of what you see today. If I could find just the right thing I could feel good about doing and being famous." He laughingly bowed before her.

"Here Mr. Garrett I love your work. Can I please have your autograph?" Emily teased as she placed a contract in front of him. "Sign here and here."

"Do you want me to add a personal note my dear?"

"Just your signature, sir. And tell all those pretty groupies to keep their mitts off my man! Initial MAG here and here and we are finished."

"Let's go to the hotel and see if we can find any of the kids. Maybe we can all eat together."

The vacation was a complete success, as the family bonded. The summer break turned out to be a huge relaxing event. The children often exclaimed at the bond they all felt. "When other families are struggling to get along, we just seem to get closer." Wesley had insightfully added during one of their nightly devotion time. Mark included that, "When you put God into the center of your life and family He controls the outcome if you let Him."

It was an enjoyable time for them all. Once back home the children prepared to go back to school. Erika, Nancy, and Edward would go back to the states and the younger children said they were ready for school to begin. In the next few days Emily decided to examine areas of the house that she had avoided.

For the entire time that Emily had been here in this house, she had not explored two places-one the basement and the other the attic. Once when they had first started exploring she had gone to the basement and found it very eerie and she and Alex had backed away and only Alex would go there when necessary. Then one day they went to the attic and Alex opened the door. Emily felt heaviness about the room and before Alex could turn on the light she backed away and said, "No." As she turned to go Alex had shut the door and took her by the arm "What is wrong?" She had told him that something just said not today within her mind. Then as their lives had grown busy the attic was forgotten. Today

I will go to the attic. Compelled by something she wasn't exactly sure why but she needed to see it. The rooms on the third floor were usually used for extra guest; all of them had a bath with each bedroom. Some of the rooms had twin beds and some had full beds. As she walked toward the end of this floor to the final stairway, she ascended the stairs she paused on the landing at the top to look at the door of the attic. Without hesitating she walked up a few stairs and opened the door. She expected the old feeling but today she just felt curiosity, as she turned on the light.

The room was filled with trunks and huge armoires. It was filled with so many items that she didn't know where to begin. Sighting a beautifully carved trunk she was drawn to start with it. She knelt, first examining the outside of the trunk and its carved details; next she opened it and inside found a letter sitting on the very top. Hesitating to open it she thought "Well it is my stuff now." Then she opened the letter and read, "*I knew that you would be drawn to this trunk. These things I have set aside for you. They belong to you. Enjoy them.*" Emily fingered the letter with its fine penmanship. The letters felt raised to the touch. It obviously had been carefully written. Was it her uncle? Of course it had to be since no one else lived here.

Inside the trunk, she found pictures wrapped carefully in a lace handkerchief. She folded the kerchief over them and laid it aside for later examination. Next was a beautiful pink hand knitted blanket. Carefully folded inside the blanket was a beautiful blue dress. These too she folded and put aside.   Next she found a quilt with hand details in the wedding ring design. Inside the quilt she discovered a smaller baby quilt. The baby quilt was pastel blue and included some very tiny baby clothes-little layettes, booties, and hats-all very carefully preserved. At the bottom of the trunk she found a beautifully carved box with what appeared to be ivory inlays. As she tenderly fingered the intriguing designs she wondered at the workmanship that had gone into making this treasure. "I love this." She opened it to find a faded rose velvet lined box. Several hankies contained carefully wrapped pieces of jewelry. "What lovely pieces." As she picked up a particularly heavy piece she found a gold watch upon unwrapping it. An engraved phrase was on the inside cover, 'To M from E. Our love will survive through eternity'

"That is very strange, but it would be a great gift for Mark." She placed it back inside the jewelry box then placed it with the other items from the trunk and closed the trunk. She gathered her finds and placed them on top of the trunk. She looked around the room she announced to the room, "I'll be back latter, for now I want to examine my finds closer."

At the back of the room she saw what looked to be a place where a window had been but then somewhere in time it had been bricked over. Walking closer to examine it, "I wonder where you come out." She picked up her treasures and ran down stairs. Placing her items in the library she ran outside to look up to where the window should be. There was a window and it still had the outside window showing.

Once back inside she was thinking how inviting the attic room would be with that window letting in light. Momentarily she wondered why it was bricked over. Her treasures were calling out to her so she went into the library and opened the curtains to let in more light. She had a feeling that she was about to discover who the M and E were. Carefully she began to examine her finds.

First the box which had all the carvings appeared to be swirls with tiny 'MLOVESE' in the middle of each swirl. The writing was a fancy calligraphy writing that blended with the swirls. At the very top inlays of ivory highlighted the M LOVES E. Around the outside of the top tiny fancy hearts outlined the other carvings. Inside each heart were tiny letters ME adorned in ivory. Beautiful carved flowers were etched on the sides of the box. Carefully she looked at the bottom of the treasure box by holding it over her head. To her amazement this was carved on the bottom, 'Especially for Em with all my love Mark.'

She placed the box on the table and backed away just staring at it as if she thought it would come alive. "What is this? Exactly who…where?" She had spoken aloud and Mark heard her from outside the room. He entered to see her standing about a foot from a lovely box. He watched quietly as she cautiously opened the box to examine its contents.

The faded red lining turned out to be a faded purple lining as she looked closer. She picked up a hankie and a handmade card fell out. She opened the card and read, "I will love you forever. Our love will transcend time. Mark"

A letter had fallen from the card when Emily opened it and after hearing what she read he crossed over and picked it up. Emily looked at him with wonder in her eyes. He opened the letter and began to read aloud, *"My precious darling Emme, I hope you will understand why I cannot be with you on this day. Our anniversary will always be a very special day for me. You are my life and without you I don't exist. I will never love anyone but you. My love grows deeper each day and I truly regret not being there to go with this part of our life together. When I heard about the baby I was surrounded by an encompassing joy. Although it makes me very happy I worry that I am not there. In my heart and dreams I am holding you in my arms. Know that our love is one that will never end. It will remain throughout all time. Take care of yourself and our little one. I will return home as soon as I am able. Please never forget that I will love you always and remember as you go to bed each night thinking of me that I am thinking of you. Your loving husband, Mark."* As he finished reading it he looked at Emily. They both looked at each other not really knowing how to feel. "Where did you get this? I didn't write it." She handed him the note from the trunk in the attic.

"This is all so weird Mark. Look at all of this. It is only part of the attic contents. I just wanted to examine these things closely."

Mark picked up the box and carefully scrutinized the carvings; the carvings and inscription on the bottom made him put it down just as Emily had done earlier. "All this was in the attic? You have never gone in the attic all this time?"

"Something always made me feel uncomfortable when I tried to go there. Alex always said that when the time was right we could explore, but as long as I said no we would consider it off limits.

"This is very strange Em."

"Well it certainly isn't something I expected."

They carefully examined each piece of jewelry and the pictures. The blue antique dress was soft hand tatted lace. It was long and extremely elegant. The quilt was a faded blue in the wedding ring design. Unfolding the quilt Emily showed him the baby clothes she had discovered.-three hand made little layettes and little boy outfits, a couple of yellow nightgowns, hand knitted sweaters, booties and hats. "These are very tiny." Emily commented holding the baby things very tenderly. While Emily held up and examined each baby item she fondled them carefully. Mark watched the expression on her face wondering if she missed her own little Robin. A fleeting thoughtful wish entered his mind …but that would not be possible because of their ages now. Concentrating on the task at hand, "This is very unsettling."

"And weird." Emily shuttered. "Look at these pictures." She unfolded the hankie with the pictures in it. Upon examining each picture a story began to unfold. The first picture was a pretty woman wearing a pretty dress and a period hat. On the back the inscription read, 'To Mark, Love Mom'. After reading it she handed it to Mark. As he looked closely at the picture Emily looked at the next one-a small woman in the dress that they had found and a taller man in a period suit. They looked very happy. On the back of this photo it read, 'Mark and Emme on their wedding day, August 9, in the year of our Lord 1914.' Mark and Emily looked at each other and at the same time said, "That is our wedding date! August 9."

Realization hit Emily at that moment, "I think I know why I never felt free to go in the attic."

Mark too was thinking the same thing, "God was keeping you from there."

"Alex did say that when the time was right I would know when to go there."

"Imagine the confusion this would have caused if you had gone earlier."

Emily felt herself feeling dizzy and sat down on the chair beside the table. Mark stood beside her and picked up the last picture of a small baby dressed in one of the little outfits they had found. On the back was written, 'Mark Allen Garrett, II.' Why are my family ancestor's things in this attic?"

"Let's see what else is in here." Emily picked up another hankie with more pictures. Another photo of a man, woman and a baby was labeled on the back-Mark, Emme, and baby Mark. "I wish I knew the story behind these pictures. We may never know."

"Maybe this will help," Emily picked up a book that said *McLeod Clan History.*

Mark opened up to the first page and read, "This is a record of the generations of the McLeod Clan. The story begins in Scotland and has been passed down through generations. The note read, *"Our wish to provide future generations with historical information and therefore enable them to add to our family history by adding their stories to the volumes of history."* Jarrod McLeod. An envelope fell to the floor and as it hit the floor Emily saw Mrs. Emily McLeod Daniels written on it in large letters. This was all creating a very 'funny' feeling in her stomach. "You read it Mark."

He looked at Emily with concern; she looked very pale, "Sweetheart, we can wait until later if you want." Mark was more interested in taking care of his wife than finding out about the attic findings. "Let's take a break and get a bite to eat."

Emily agreed and they went to the kitchen for lunch. Emily assured Mark that she was weak because of the need to eat. They talked while at the table, "You need to look at the attic. There is so much stuff in it. Oh and there is this brick wall at the end that looks like a window was bricked up. If it could be opened it would let in so much light."

Mark started laughing and said, "She's back!" They laughed and made plans to go to the library and continue reading the letter. After they both had eaten they felt refreshed and the curious findings were now easier to examine.

Upon returning to the library Mark picked up the letter and began to read, *"Emily I am your great uncle if you are reading this then I have died. I prayed that God would let you find this only when the time is right. My part of the family history has been completed. I am entrusting you with the family history from this point. Add your story to my story. I chose you my sweet Emily to be my heiress for many reasons that I hope will become clearer as you read this book. You were chosen because your name has a special meaning to me. I cannot explain it because these things have always puzzled me, but there is a bond here that has developed in our lineage. You were my choice even if you chose not to come here. My instructions were to be sure you got the trunk. But if you are here then the trunk was to be left in the attic for you to find when God led you there. Please read the book to discover the story. I pray that God will always keep you safe and happy,"*

Mark paused and looked at Emily as she sat there quietly trying to comprehend everything. "Do you want me to continue?"

"Yes Mark, Let's read it." She pointed at the book.

"Honey, this may very well be 'Our History' not just yours. You look pretty shaken,"

She closed her eyes and sat back in the chair. Then she opened them and looked at Mark and together they said, "We were meant to be together. God doesn't make mistakes!"

He drew her up into his arms, "God put us together. For all that we have been through and through all of our pain of loss it is so clear that God directed our paths. My precious Emily I will love you for the rest of my life."

Leaning on Mark she looked up into his eyes and said "I believe that too. Mark we belong together."

They stood together for a while contemplating the day's findings. Mark took her face in his hands and gently kissed her. Looking at her husband she said, "You know it's really funny that I never even wanted to go near the attic until today. This morning all I could think about was going to the attic. Before I always felt like I would suffocate when I tried to go there. I found the trunk and even looked around a bit before I came down here. I went outside to see where the window I told you about would be. You know the outside window is still there glass and all. You know that big room would make a nice office if that window was opened."

"When you get ideas in your head, I know what I will be doing." Mark laughed.

She picked up the book and handed it to Mark. Upon opening the book they sat down beside each other at the table. Mark said, "Emily I think we just may be connected in some way."

"I hope we aren't related." She laughed.

The next few pages were family trees that started in the 1500s. The detail and amount of information showed the meticulous work that had gone in to keeping this history up to date. It was amazing how it had been preserved. While turning the page some loose paper fell out. On these pages were family trees with the name Garrett at the top. Emily's family tree was there and her name and her grandfather, Jasper, and her father, Samuel were all circled. On Mark's family tree the names Joshua, and Alice were circled. A note was attached-Joshua Garrett married Alice Edwards they had the following children-Alexander, twins-Nathan and Edward, Mark Allen, and Allie. Mark Allen married Emme Lucille McLeod, daughter of my brother Charles, Jr. who married Martha Edwards (Alice's cousin). Emme and Mark had a son, Mark Allen II. Their complete story can be found in chapter 12 of this volume.

"Mark we need to read all of this."

"It could take months to research every part of it but I believe we are connected."

"You read I will listen."

Both of them agreed to turn directly to chapter 12 to read the Garrett story.

Mark began reading, "Charles, Jr. and his lifetime friend Joshua Garrett left Scotland to go work in the mines near England. The met cousins Alice and Martha Edwards and Joshua married Alice and Charles, Jr. my oldest brother married Martha. Within a few years Alice had given birth to Alex, Edward and Nathan the twins, Mark Allen and little Allie. After trying a few years Charles and Martha gave birth to Evan and Emily, but through a mix up in recording Emily's name was listed as Emme. An accident at the mines occurred and both Joshua and Charles died. Martha and Alice decided to keep their families together and Martha went to work in the mines while Alice kept the children. Latter Martha became ill and died. Alice needing help wrote to my lifelong friend Mark Columcil Garrett to ask for help and to inform him that I needed to come for my niece and nephew. We left Scotland and went for the children. Mark and I took care of both Martha and her children. We returned and built Alice a home between our two houses. I paid her to watch Emme and Evan while I worked. Evan became ill with pneumonia and died leaving me with only my little Emme, of whom I became very fond. Mark and I had gone into business together and we were doing very well, not rich, but we were comfortable. Mark met and married Molly Taylor. Molly was from a poor family whose parents had left for Australia promising to return for the children. This left the children to fend for themselves. Molly's sister found a position with a wealthy family. She was more than happy to have Molly marry. I became a close friend to Alice and had planned to ask her to marry me, but I was too late. A rich man from America, Alexander Graham Daniels, after knowing her only two weeks asked her to marry him. She apologized to me and told me that her heart would always belong to me, but Alexander had offered her a new way of life for her and the children. In those days women had no rights so she felt that it was the best for her children. She left for America and I never saw her or her children again."

"Mark, do you think that her Alex and my Alex are related?"

"I don't know…this is getting very strange and confusing. I think I have a huge knot in my stomach."

"Me too. It is strange. Is there any more?"

"Yes apparently this book is full of stories. Are you sure you want me to continue."

Emily nodded and Mark began again, "I was devastated after Alice left. Apparent that all those for whom I cared were now gone. At first I had thought of going after Alice in America, but realized that it would only cause her pain. Mark's wife watched Emme while I worked. As Emme grew older she became very beautiful. Various men came to court her, but she turned them all away saying that the only man she would ever accept had to be as good as her Uncle Jarrod.

In the summer of her fifteenth birthday Mark's nephew Mark Allen came to live with them. He was sixteen and he and Emme had an instant bond. Mark Allen obtained a position as apprentice in a local firm. He advanced very fast and a year later on his seventeenth birthday he proposed to Emme. She was sixteen and in those days that was considered a good age to be married. They had a very happy year but in the second year Mark Allen was sent to America on a trip. He worked for a firm that had holdings in both America and Australia. Shortly after he left Emme found that she was pregnant. Mark came home in time for Emme to present baby Mark to his father. Baby Mark was the tiniest baby I had ever seen, but the joy this little family had was hard to describe. Then Mark's company told him he would be sent to Australia. After he arrived he decided to buy land there. He wrote to Emme and wanted her to join him. She had already become pregnant again and wanted to go so she didn't tell me. I refused to let her go alone so I sold my business and my lands. Mark C. and Molly also sold theirs and decided to join us. We boarded the ship and began the voyage it was on the voyage that I first learned of Emme's pregnancy. She had a rough trip and upon our arrival Emme was told that Mark had been in an accident and died. I had bought some land and a business. But Emme mourned so much that it sent her into early labor. She and her baby died shortly after birth. Little Mark mourned for his mom and soon became sick and died three months later. I had three graves on my new property. Mark and Molly had also bought land and a business in Sydney where Molly found her parents. I decided to move on after donating my land to a local church with the stipulation that their graves be always attended. I finally settled here and started a business and bought this land. I never married. Love was not to ever be mine in this life, but I was happy and my cherished memories of my little Emme were enough to bring joy to my life. Although I never had a child of my own, Emme was given to me by God to raise and love as my own. God always sustained me and led me in the paths that I should go. Please always remember that God alone has a perfect plan for us. –Jarrod McLeod."

"Oh Mark do you think he was really happy? I don't think I could live without love."

"He trusted God and he did live to be a very old man. And what an empire he built. It was as if he built it for you. He definitely let God lead his life. You need to start a new volume and continue this story. Tell about your own story."

"It will be 'our story' Mark."

"You are my story my sweet Emily."

"Is there more written?"

"Yes there are a few more entries." Mark began reading, "*January, 1977. I have been sick for the last few years so I felt it necessary to put things in order. My goal is to take care of those I love and who have cared for me all these years. I and my brother, Jasper are the last of my immediate family. Some years ago my brother's son Samuel came to visit me and showed me pictures of his young daughter Emily. She was a very pretty girl and reminded me of my own Emme. My heart jumped with excitement at the thought of her. My lawyer friend has taken on research to find if they are still alive and well. Not having any children I plan to choose an heir from these my closest relatives."*

Mark paused to add, "This looks like where he found you." Mark pointed out a genealogy tree on her family. He turned the page and found a page of his own family tree. "I understand why he was looking for you but why did he look for me?"

"Read some more Mark. Maybe there will be answers."

Mark continued, "Here is another entry on March 1978."

"Jasper is not living, but Samuel is still living. He is a minister and his daughter, Emily Lucille is still living. After finding them I decided to track down Mark C. Garrett's son and found that he had a young son named curiously enough to me, Mark Allen. In my findings I found that he was my nearest neighbor only about a couple of miles away. His land is next to my land. I am thinking maybe our two families belong together somehow our lives are entwined."

"Wow this is so unsettling, but it has incited my interest. He was really smooth. We came here often and the way he found out about me was from me. He always seemed so interested in me."

"Is there more?"

Mark nodded and continued, *"I have decided that it is only appropriate that my great niece should be my heiress. She has my precious Emme's name and she will have to decide to come here. I will take care of her but my wish is for her to come in order to have it all. I am not playing match maker but I wish for her to meet young Mark to at least become friends. Both she and Mark have happy families but I feel that our two families are meant to stay close. So I hope that they can all become close friends. I leave it in God's hands and I know that His plans are always the best. If He wishes it my prayer is this will be a blest friendship."*

Mark stopped and looked at Emily, "Whew! My heart is in my throat.|"

"Is that the end?"

"No there is a bit more." Mark then read once more, *"I am very tired and must sleep. This will most likely be my last family tree entry. I have left detailed instructions for how my estate is to be handled. If Emily comes for the allotted time she will have it all, but in case she chooses not to come the trunk will be sent to her. If she comes it will be placed in the attic awaiting her to find. My prayer is that she will come."*

"That is it. He wanted us to meet and now more than ever I see God's hand in our meeting. We aren't kin but we are connected through the past."

"We were meant to meet."

"Em, we are connected, in mind, spirit, and body. It all points to one thing. We write "Our Story" using this as a plot."

"Do you think it could sell?"

"Yes baby I do. It must also include how God works in mysterious ways."

Mark smiled at her and then wanted to assure her that he only wanted her to think about it. "I don't mean to use your family history as a stepping stone to making money."

"It is our family histories Mr. Garrett. I look forward to doing a little bit more research and then we can write it together. We have a great deal of work ahead of us." Glancing up toward the attic she said, "I know just the place to begin, both researching mental and physical."

Mark shook his head, "I know the attic!"

"It will be great; you will see."

They took Emily's finds and put them away then arm in arm they went up to the attic. "We can't really start something new until we start on your project." Mark teased her. "First, Mrs. Garrett I suggest a break." He pulled her toward the bedroom. She smiled and they gently shut the door.

Later as they opened the attic door, "Mark I wonder if the past really repeats itself."

"Maybe this comes out of context, but the Bible does say that there is nothing new under the sun." He grinned, "The fact that this history has similarities to our lives, we have our own moments in time.

Everything depends on the feelings we have inside. Men seem to make the same mistakes, but God is there with a pure love to guide us."

"Still it is strange about our names being the same. There are times when I don't think I understand anything." Turning to face him she leaned against his chest, "I do know one thing."

Placing his hand on her hair, "What's that?"

"I know that I love you and I know that God has put us together. More than any other thing I will always love you."

"Many things have made an impression on our lives, Alex and Robyn gave us love and we lost both of them. God never promised any of us that things would be perfect but He did say that He would be there to go with us through the storm."

They sat on two of the chairs in the attic and Mark continued, "God gave us his strength to be able to stand. Baby, there were times after Robyn died that I envied you and Alex. I had to pray every day to keep Satan in the form of envy away." He reached out and brushed a twig of hair from her face, "I wasn't going to ever tell you this but Alex came to me after you were given peace from your dreams. He and I both had been having the dreams." His expression was so pained that it scared her. "On the day he came to see me he asked me to take care of you if anything happened to him."

"That was Alex he always wanted to be sure I was okay."

"Honey what he asked of me that day was more than just general care. He asked me to please love you."

Emily looked at this man kneeling in front of her. Her heart swelled with emotion and tears rolled down her cheeks. "He loved me that much? More than that, he loved you enough to ask that of you."

He reached out pulling her up from the chair and enfolded her into his arms. "It wasn't hard to do. I can say that after Alex died I found that I already loved you. We are so very blessed."

They stayed there for a while. Both of them felt so wonderfully blessed by God.

"Listen!" Mark looked up.

"I don't hear anything."

"You don't hear that?" he grinned and in a falsetto voice, *"Mark, Emily get busy cleaning the attic."*

They laughed and tussled a little. "We have things to do the kids will be here soon."

Mark watched her as he began thinking '*My beautiful little wife will you ever know how deeply I love you.*' Almost as if she felt him thinking about her she turned and stared at him. For a moment they just stared at each other. Emily sensed him looking at her and somehow she could feel his love reaching out to her. At first she thought she had heard him speak but when she looked at him he was quiet. . Mark was first to look away. "Where do we start?"

"Here." She reached out and kissed him, "I just now realized how much a part of me you are. I felt myself be loved and turned to see you staring at me."

"We have become one. It is inspiring and all encompassing."

They both knew that this was God's will and more than anything they knew they were meant to be together.

CHAPTER
ELEVEN

~

"Look Em, this old hat box is full of old pictures." Mark held up some pictures.

She joined him and they sat on the floor looking through the pictures, "Look they all have names and dates on them.

"You know how Nancy and Erika like to scrap-book maybe they will like cataloging these by date."

"Hey Em, this is my grandfather. "It looks like …but according to the date it isn't. Wow. It sure looks like him."

"There are so many things here that we can add to our story." She looked around the room. "This room can be our writing room."

"Yes it will be perfect. That is if we ever get finished cleaning it."

They continued working with Mark moving some of the trunks and boxes. Emily sat on the floor in front of one of the trunks. "Look Mark more pictures." Mark came over to see her find. "Hey how about a break? Hank and Leigha are supposed to be coming at one. We could take a lunch break."

"I guess so and I have been sitting in one place too long. The other kids will be here soon."

Mark wiped the sweat from his forehead and offered her a hand, "We have been at it all morning."

As Mark helped her stand to her feet, she felt a wave of nausea and then she was dizzy.

"Mark reached out to steady her and noticed that she was extremely pale, "What's wrong?"

"I guess I have been sitting in one place too long and got up too fast."

"You need to eat too. Here lean on me."

"Really I am fine. Just getting old I guess, after all Grandpa, I am a Grandma." She laughed and turned to walk away and then everything went dark. Mark caught her just as she fell. Lifting her up, he headed down the stairs just as Hank and Leigha paused on the landing. "Open that door," He ordered. Leigha opened the door and Mark gently laid her on the small bed. "She fainted, Hank get a wet cloth from bathroom." Mark then placed it on her forehead. Emily stirred and looked up into Mark's worried face. "What happened?"

"You fainted; just stay down for a bit."

"Non-sense I am fine." She got up and suddenly pushed them aside, "Excuse me..." and headed to the bathroom. Mark following close behind her saw his wife become very sick.

Once assured that she was not going to pass out again, he turned to see Hank and Leigha who were smiling and he was shocked at their lack of empathy. Emily came back into the room, "Honey, Hank and I can finish in the attic for today. I think you should rest and call Dr. Gordon. This is the third time you have been sick this week." Mark sat her down on the bed and began washing her face. He looked at Hank and Leigha who obviously were amused by the situation. "I don't think this is funny you guys. She could have a virus. Have a heart, she's sick!"

"Mom, do you have anything to tell us...Especially Mark. Just look at him Mom. He is terrified." She looked at her mom with knowing eyes.

"Yes Mark, I will call Dr. Gordon, and there is a possibility I do know what is wrong."

She smiled at Mark and patted his hand, who remained bewildered. Emily thought with five children that he would figure it out. But their ages probably kept both of them believing they were too old. When she realized that he was really upset she said, "Sweetheart, don't be so worried." He stood up and gathered her into his arms and held her close. It was obvious he was having difficulty speaking. At this moment all he could think about was what if this was something that would take her from him.

"Baby it is okay." Sensing his unrealistic worry, she tried to sooth him as she added, "There is a possibility we will be adding one more to our family." Smiling and touching her stomach.

As the statement penetrated his mind he looked at her incredulously. "You are nearly forty and well how…?"

"Dad I think you do know how." Hank let out a big laugh and patted his father's shoulder. "Or do you have something to tell us kids."

For the moment no one existed but his precious wife. "I love you. I never thought we would have a baby now at our age. Our love made this…" He patted her stomach.

"Well love, let us be sure first. It could be a virus." She teased.

"Yeah, like it will take a few months to find a cure." Leigha laughed.

"Yep, Leigha had that same virus, but Jeremiah was the cure."

They all laughed and went downstairs. After lunch they talked about the baby and about finishing the attic. Emily felt fine and busied herself looking through the old photos. Hank and Mark were in the attic gently removing bricks from the closed up window. Since you could see the window complete with glass from the outside they were careful with the removal. Mark decided to save the old bricks in case they could be reused. Looking at the brick in his hand and then at his son, "This old mansion has so many rooms but Emily chose this one, because it 'has character' you know." He winked.

"You know Dad that you could have hired someone to do the work for you. It's not like you don't have any money." He held up his hands to stop Mark's comment, "I know. I know. 'But there isn't any fun in that'."

Mark started talking as if things had finally sunk in, "Hank, a baby!" Mark shook his head in wonder. "I wanted a baby with her, but I just figured that it wasn't going to happen. Our ages you know."

"Well, Dad I guess it has finally sunk in." Hank patted his dad's shoulder, "I am surprised you didn't think it possible. After all, you have been very fertile, six kids dad."

"But Alex and Emily tried so long after Emily and nothing until little Robin. I just thought our child bearing years were over."

"It's great Dad, but it might be a bit confusing for him or her."

"How do you figure that?"

"This baby will be my half sibling and my in law too."

"I hadn't thought about that one. Well it will be one for the family history books."

Mark turned back to his work. Hank watched his Dad with pride thinking how young he looked for his age. He had only a few grey hairs around his sideburns and Emily had none. In fact Emily still looked young enough to be Leigha's sister. Time had been very good to them.

"Hey Dad, I think it is great that our family is so close. As time goes by we all seem to grow closer. I am thankful that you have raised us in a Christian home. If I can be half the Dad to Jeremiah that you have been to me, he will be okay."

"God makes all the difference in our lives. The main thing to remember is to let Him lead and give Him first place. Teach Jeremiah to love the Lord. You just have to let the Lord lead."

"Dad, I love you. You know we don't say it enough. You and Mom and now Emily have been a true blessing to me. God gave me Leigha." He grinned, "A guy couldn't ask for more."

"You are right son. We don't say it enough. I love you too." They smiled at each other and continued working. Suddenly there was light as they uncovered the window.

"Hey look at that." Mark and Hank were laughing and congratulating each other, when Emily, Leigha and Ariel entered. They all looked around the room and expressed how cheery that one window light changed it. They all began working in various areas of the attic. Hank and Ariel were busy removing the bricks and taking them downstairs. Mark stopped occasionally to watch Emily part in amazement of her and part in feelings of unending love. Emily stopped and looked at him too. She could feel him loving her. She really wanted to have a baby with him. She went back to sorting things in the trunk she was kneeling beside. Mark came over and touched her shoulder. "Maybe you should go down and rest. You need to take care of yourself."

"I am fine sweetie."

"Wesley and Louis will be up in a few minutes. They are changing clothes and they can help finish up."

"When they get here I will go down. Now, please stop worrying about me. I will be fine."

"Mom, are you sick again?" Ariel entered and overheard the last of their conversation.

"Hello, little girl." Mark hugged her and said, "Mom is fine didn't you hear her say that."

"Yes, but I also heard the concern in your tone. I was there yesterday when she got sick."

"Mom is going to have a baby." Hank told her. She looked at Mark and then at her mother. "Mark I am speechless and Mom, you don't need to be up here. You should be resting." Ariel stomped her foot and put her hands on her hips.

"Hey little one she will be fine and we aren't going to let her overdo." Hank teased Ariel always calling her little one.

"Hank I am not a little girl."

"You aren't getting any bigger so you'll always be a little girl to me."

"Not everyone is ten feet tall!" She stuck her tongue out at him.

Mark was watching and marveled at how much like Emily Ariel was. She was petite with bright eyes that sparkled when she talked. She had Alex's eyes but her personality was all Emily.

"Ariel, Mom will be just fine." Leigha assured her.

"Hey everybody Dr. Gordon is downstairs. He came to see Emily." Wesley entered with Louis right behind him.

"Emily what is wrong are you sick?" Louis looked worried. He like Mark worried about Emily. "Nothing is wrong with you is it?"

Patting his cheek, "I am fine and nothing is wrong."

"Mark did you call him?" Emily asked.

"No, Mom I did." Leigha confessed. "After all we want no worries."

"I could have seen him tomorrow."

"I know but when I called, he said he was coming out this way and would stop by."

Wesley and Louis stood by her side. Wesley asked, "Are you sure you are okay?" Dr. Gordon scared him mainly because it made him think about the night his Mom died. Emily sensed his apprehension and so she whispered in his ear. "I might be pregnant or it might be a virus." She kissed his cheek. "Be careful for us." He hugged her. Emily nodded and then turned to go down to see the doctor.

"Will someone please tell me what's going on?" Louis demanded. "Just because I am the youngest…" Mark told him and at the bottom of the stairs she heard him yell, "That's great Emily." Then he turned back to Mark and said, "Way to go Dad."

After the doctor examined her, he called Mark and Emily into the library. "I took some blood samples and a specimen. But from all that I can find from my exam I believe you are pregnant. I will call you as soon as your labs are done. Right now I want to assure you both that your age is a factor but you both are healthy active individuals. I see no reason that this pregnancy should not go well. Since you have been pregnant before you know the precautions and care you need to have. Be smart and take care of yourself. You, Mark take care of her… but I know you will." Everyone was waiting to hear the news as Dr. Gordon left. "Thank you for coming out, Dr. Gordon." Mark shook his hand and after he left Mark turned to see questioning eyes staring at him. "Everyone come into the library." Once everyone was seated Mark began, "I want to begin with a scripture, (The earth is the Lords and everything that is in it." Psalm 24:1) We as a family have been totally blessed in that now Emily and I are to be blessed by another child." They were all smiling and saying congratulations; then Mark held up his hand for attention, "We are humbled by the blessings of God. So at this moment I think we all need to take some time to thank Him and ask his blessing upon this new life." They all knelt and Mark led in prayer over the new baby and over the whole family. He asked that they all be instrumental in this child's life. They would bring the baby up to know the Lord. It was a solemn but happy occasion. As they went upstairs to clean up and get ready for dinner, Emily and Mark went into the kitchen and told Kate, Pam, Betty, and Becky the news. The Lord was good and greatly to be praised.

"Sometimes God lets us know that He approves of our choices. He has blessed us beyond my imagination by giving us a child." Mark said once he an Emily went to their room and for the moment the time was theirs alone.

"I believe with all my heart that sometimes God says our time is up and then at other times He puts His stamp of approval on our choices. He has shown His approval of us, by sending us the blessing of life." Emily patted her stomach as Mark drew her into his arms.

After dinner was over everyone gathered in the library for the nightly devotion. Hank asked if it would be okay if he led the devotion for tonight. He began with a beautiful passage from Ephesians 2:8-9 "For by grace are we saved through faith, it is the gift of God…Not of works lest any man should boast." I chose these scriptures to remind us of God's amazing grace in the light of our blessings from above I want each of us to remember who has saved us and from where our blessings come. As long as we always remember where we are and that it is God's grace that leads us we will always have His peace. May we as a family take it upon ourselves to follow God's path and know that He is with us."

After prayer everyone told Hank that he chose the perfect devotional. As they were leaving to go to bed for the night, Hank asked Mark if he could talk to him. Emily excused herself and went to the attic to look around. She found that it was clean and ready for more exploration. As she was contemplating how this day had been truly a blessing, "Peace I leave you." She could hear the Lord's speaking to her. "*Thank you, Lord for all your blessings. Help me to always search for You and follow your path.*"

Hearing a movement behind her she turned to find Hank, Leigha and Mark standing there. "We don't want to intrude on your prayer."

"That's fine I was just thanking God."

"Well, I have more news to share with you." Hank came over and lifted her to her feet then he put his arm around Emily. "I have decided to listen to God. He has called me into His ministry."

Emily reached up and hugged him and tears flooded her eyes. "Hank, that is wonderful. It will be hard, but it will also be a blessing."

"Grandpa has been talking with us about this," He motioned for Leigha to join him. "We are going to live with them while I attend the seminary."

It was a happy time but also sad to see them going so far away. Emily knew that she had to relinquish them to live their own life and follow what God's path for them contained.

Blessings from God and decisions to follow God's path led to peaceful repose. When your eyes are on God, He gives a peaceful understanding as you lean on Him, giving to Him your life.

CHAPTER
TWELVE

～

The morning brought a new beginning for the family as they returned to the attic. The boys finished taking the old bricks from the window down to Larry who used them to finish a path around the flower garden in front of the house. The attic was ready for Emily's designs which she had tacked up on the wall. There were two other windows at the back that had shutters on them. Emily commented that they would let in more light. "Hank and I will take the shutters off."

"Wait" Emily crossed over to the window lifted it and found a latch which released the shutters and they could easily be opened and fastened to the wall from inside. She turned and faced the others. She realized that she didn't know how she knew how to do that.

"How did you know how to do that?" Mark asked.

"I don't know. I must have read it somewhere." She shrugged her shoulders.

"You read it? I see," Mark joked looking at her he sensed she didn't want to continue the conversation.

"There is also another window on the other side of the room. It is behind that large armoire." Emily was seeking to change the subject. Mark looked at her with a question on his lips, but stopped short of asking it. A feeling came over him and he didn't understand it but he could feel her discomfort. He motioned to Hank to help him move the armoire. While trying to move it Emily said, "It might be easier if you take the books out first.'"

"What books?" Wesley asked, as Mark opened the doors and found it to be full of volumes of books. Everyone crowded around and started taking books and putting them on the floor. After the armoire was empty Mark and Hank easily moved the armoire to the other side. Another large window was there and had been covered with a large piece of plywood. Mark took it down and more bright light poured in lighting the room so much that more details of the room was revealed.

"Look Mark." Emily pointed at the top of the room where there was the alphabet and under it was wallpaper with red and blue lines. "It was a school room."

"I can see why." Leigha said, "It is bright and cheerful here."

Emily was so excited and bubbly; her excitement was contagious and Mark reached out and hugged her.

"I can't wait to start decorating this room. It is perfect for a writing room."

"Just don't overdo." Mark smiled and patted her stomach.

Grinning at him she went over and picked up one of the books. As she read the cover title "Oh my," she exclaimed. Everyone crowded around as she read it aloud, "McLeod Family History 1790-1800."

"Emily the book we were reading downstairs said that the histories went back to the 1500s. Maybe the first one is here." Mark sat down on the floor and began looking through the books. "I found it the first one." Mark held up the book for Emily to see. With peeked interest the children started organizing the volumes of history.

"These are really old." Ariel observed. "We need to be very careful with them."

Ariel had always loved family history and antiques too. She and Alex used to go antiquing.

"Look Mom this isn't a historical volume. It looks like an old reader. They are beginning readers and on through advanced readers." Nancy excitedly held up a reader.

Leigha who loved old books became excited and started rummaging through the old books, "These in this pile are original prints." She exclaimed.

"There are all types of books here. You know I think this may have been a school room."

Leigha said. "Here are some literature and some history, and an old science book."

Everyone began opening the other armoires. Inside one armoire was old clothes, shoes, and hat boxes. "Oh Mark these are full of story ideas. What a perfect writing room."

"These old things and the histories will keep us busy." Mark added.

He noticed Emily looking a bit tired and said, "I think we need to go get ready for supper. We all could use a good shower." Mark smelled Ariel knowing she was the one who worried most about body odor, "Yes I think some of us really need to stop for tonight." Poking Ariel playfully he started laughing.

"Mark I know just where Hank gets his love of tormenting me!" She pretended to pout.

"Tomorrow we can get organized and start decorating." Hank said.

Ariel said, "Why don't you just hire someone to do it?"

"Well why spend the money when we have so many able bodies here." Hank laughed.

"Besides we would miss out on all the fun." Emily reminded them.

They all came down for supper after getting clean. As they were around the table, the phone rang and Mark went to answer it. Everyone was laughing when Mark reentered the room. He was unusually quiet. They all sat down to eat. Emily had been the only one to notice Mark's expression. He obviously was very upset about something. When he worried it seemed his eyes turned a clearer blue. She decided not to ask about the call at this moment, because his mouth was tightly drawn and he looked more worried than angry. He glanced at Hank and Wesley and they too decided not to ask. But just as Hank was going to suggest they retire to the library Ariel the worrier asked, "Who was on the phone?"

"Dr. Gordon," Mark replied. He looked at Emily as if he didn't want to look anywhere else. Actually he was trying desperately not to look worried in front of the children. When anything was wrong she was his strength and he could usually sense it if she worried. "He and Sara will be here to see us."

Hank suggested that they all go into the library. Leigha started to ask what the doctor had said when Hank put his finger on his lips. Ariel still wanted to know more but Wesley and Louis led her away. She finally noticed that Mark had not taken his eyes off of her mother. They didn't even acknowledge that everyone had left the room. Mark's worry had him paralyzed as he just sat and stared at Emily. All he was thinking was "*Why God?*"

"Mark, talk to me and tell me what is wrong." She looked desperately at her husband. He got up and crossed to her chair and lifted her to her feet. Worry filled his eyes as he pulled her into his arms.

"He only said that he wanted to tell us together in person. He is bringing Sara and I just figured it was bad news."

"Mark Allen Garrett! I am surprised at you. Why are you thinking the worse? God knows what is best for us and no matter what we will face it together with Him by our side."

She searched her thoughts and feelings, but she still had a good feeling about the pregnancy. No ominous feelings lurked in her mind. Her only feelings at the moment were for her husband's worry.
Mark sensed her calmness and pulled her into his arms and said quietly, "Maybe it's nothing."

"God has been so good to us and I don't think it's bad." She snuggled into his arms feeling safe and somehow she knew things were alright. "I love you Mark and you'll see-it will be okay."

"Em we will be fine no matter what and I am sorry for thinking negatively. I remember from where fear and negativity comes-the enemy-Satan. God has not given us a spirit of fear, but of deliverance. We will be okay because God is with us. I just never want to lose you my sweet little wife. I could never handle that."

"I feel the same way honey."

"We have been through a lot of pain and loss but God has given us a great deal of love and joy." He broke into a smile that always made her heart skip a beat as his dimples showed. He looked into her big brown eyes and as she joined him in a smile they felt a renewed sense of calm. "As long as we have God here," pointing to his heart, "we will always have success."

"When we give God control and let Him have first place, we have an anchor that keeps us from drifting away." Emily assured him.

"Let us join the kids. They are probably worried too." Mark suggested. "Especially Ariel."

They joined the others to find them sitting quietly. "What's going on?" Ariel asked.

"We leave and you are upset but then you come in smiling." Wesley commented.

"What did the doctor say?" Hank asked.

"He wants to tell us in person. We feel that it will be good news, although I allowed Satan to scare me at first by thinking negatively, I know that God is in control and He will be the one who decides." Mark assured them. "We love you all and just remember that it is God who controls the future and we need to let Him lead." Mark grinned and reminded his children, "For we walk by faith and not by sight." 2 Corinthians 5:7."

The children were amazed at the faith of their parents. "Thanks Dad, if I can learn to be half the man you are then I know, I will be useful to God as a minister." Hank smiled with great respect at his father. His siblings looked at him with amazement.

"Minister? When did you decide that?" Wesley asked.

"That is so you." Edward added patting his brother on the back.

"Leigha you are going to be a pastor's wife." Nancy hugged her sister.

Ariel and Louis just stared at him. Erika hugged her brother but remained quiet.

The children led by Emily started to examine the photos from one of the hat boxes from the attic that Leigha had brought down. She was busy thinking about how calm her mother was and hoped that she could be like Emily someday. By the time Dr. Gordon and Sara arrived the children were calm and laughing over some of the photos. When the doorbell rang, Kate let the Gordons in and led them to the library.

The children had jumped when the doorbell rang, but their parents had remained calm.

Upon entering the library, Mark and Emily noticed the smiles on their faces so they figured it was good news. "Well Bob, I think you have kept us wondering long enough so out with it." Mark teased him.

Sara jabbed Bob in the side, "I told you that you would have them all worried with this 'I will tell you when I get there.' So get on with it."

"Well, Sara here needed a dress and so I thought I would bring her out and bring you the news at the same time."

"And…" Mark held his hand out in a questioning fashion.

"You better sit down,"

"Hey are you daft! I am sitting." The mood was still calm and amusing.

"You and Emily are going to have a new addition to the family. As well as a new grandchild." He grinned at Leigha.

"What? When? How?" Hank questioned.

"Hey Hank I think you would know how?" Mark teased him remembering Hank's answer to his own question when he first suspected Emily's condition.

Leigha was smiling quietly, Hank was now kneeling in front of her, "Why didn't you say anything?"

"I went to Dr. Gordon's the day before Mom's ordeal. I just wanted to be sure before I said anything."

Hank reached up smiling and kissed his wife. "I love you sweetie."

"Well Mark it looks like this house will soon hear the pitter patter of lots of little feet."

Bob teased them.

"Is there anything extra that we need to do? You know in our case, because of our age." Mark asked.

"Yes a few. Emily is underweight and a bit anemic. I brought some supplements for you to take. Due to your age we will need to take extra care. I have made appointments with an obstetrician in Melbourne for you to see. He specializes in care of older women who are pregnant. One thing you have going for you is that this isn't your first pregnancy. But in the light of little Robin's ordeal we need to keep a close eye on you.

He will come to town on certain days. This will keep you from having to go into Melbourne for checkups. I am just a general practitioner, and Dr. Henry is a specialist. We are friends and we can work closely with each other. I have set up an appointment with him for you Emily for next week at my office. I want to get this care started immediately."

Emily smiled at Mark who said, "Well, this baby is a gift from God and as far as taking good care of her… there is nothing I would not do for her. You see, Doc, I never want to lose her."

"Okay." Emily looked at Sara "Shall we go to the sewing room? I have a couple of designs that I prepared last night." Emily always hated being the center of attention and found it very uncomfortable. So she thought by changing the subject she could direct the conversation away from herself. Hugging Leah she said, "You come too."

"She probably knew that she needed designs last night." Mark joked. She turned around and gave him a look that he knew immediately to change the subject.

Although Sara and Bob had known them for years they were not close friends. Sara was a bit puzzled by Mark's comment. "What was that all about?"

Leigha knew that her mother's premonitions always embarrassed her mom, so she quickly said, "No big deal. Mom just seems to know when to design clothes. Maybe not for whom but always she knows exactly what they want."

"Enough about me Leigha, Sara I did draw these designs last night." She took out her sketch book and showed Sara her designs.

Sara looked at the drawings and then looked at Leigha, "I see what you mean."

"Just what you were thinking, right?" Leigha said.

"Yes as a matter of fact, it is." Sara looked at Emily with amazement and a new curiosity.

"Enough you two!" Emily stopped them and began taking measurements. "Leigha there are some other designs in that other book you might want to see."

Leigha looked at the designs and then at her Mom. She grinned "It figures."

They all laughed and Emily showed them the fabrics she had on hand and then a book with other fabric choices. While they were making choices the men were in the library making plans for a trip to Melbourne. Once more the future looked peaceful and the family looked forward to the upcoming births of the new little lives that would soon add to their number.

CHAPTER
THIRTEEN

The weeks passed and the family continued working on the attic room. Soon it became the writing room and Emily and Mark spent quite a few hours poring through the family histories and finding more on both his and Alex's histories. While they were busy writing, both Emily and Leigha had been preparing for their new arrivals. Nancy, Edward and Erika had returned home from the states and the whole family was also getting ready for the new arrivals. Hank and Leigha were getting ready to move to Arkansas to live with Grandma and Grandpa while Hank attended seminary. It would be sad to see them go, but Emily knew that God had to come first.

Their house would be cared for by Rosa while they were away. At this moment Hank had felt it was God's calling that he return and start a mission here. The church where they attended was small and Hank thought he might be able to help build it.

The baby would be born in America and that part saddened both she and Mark. But as soon as she and the new baby were able they planned a trip to the states. Erika would finish her nursing course in the fall and planned to return to work for Dr. Gordon. Nancy and Edward were going on to Veterinarian school, after they were married and return here to open a Veterinary Clinic. This fall Wesley and Ariel would graduate high school and Louis would graduate the next year.

Life was developing in a timely fashion and each day they always remembered to thank God for His blessings. Emily had stopped her writing to think about all these things and was deep in thought when Mark came in with coffee and a snack for her.

"Mrs. Garrett, I believe you have been working all morning and our little one is crying for hunger." Mark teased.

"Well thank the Lord this baby has a Daddy that can hear his cries. I hope that continues after the birth." She laughed.

"You know baby, this family is going through a great deal of change. Our grown children are coming and going and starting their own lives. We are going to have a new grandbaby, and a new baby of our own, Does it ever scare you just a little?"

"Mark, who gives us fear?"

"I know and I let him in sometimes, but that's one of the reasons I keep you around-to remind me to trust the Lord." He tickled her a bit.

"You are hopeless Mr. Garrett. But I love you, so I guess I will keep you."

They laughed then after eating their snack they went to work on their writing again. In the middle of the work, Emily sat straight up in her chair and yelled. "Ouch!"

Mark jumped up and ran to her side. "Em what's wrong?"

"It is this little one I think we have a soccer player here." She laughed rubbing her belly. Mark leaned over and rubbed her tummy and as he did the baby kicked his hand.

"Oh my goodness! He is a strong one."

"Could be a she you know."

"Yes it could, I just figured with my track record it would be a he."

"Well there are a few males around here." She laughed at him and playfully punched his arm. "We need more girls."

"You are pushing it mam."

They were busy joking around and had not noticed Nancy and Edward at the door.

They were watching in amusement at their parents lively banter. They both loved seeing their happiness.

"Mom if you two would work more and play less you wouldn't have to stay up here all the time." Nancy pretended to be mad.

"Well what brings you two to our writing room?" Mark asked.

"Dad we would like to talk to you both. You know that we will finish our initial courses in the fall, but we would like to attend a veterinary school here in Australia instead of staying in the states."

"Have you checked to see where one might be?"

"The School of Veterinary Medicine is the ninth most famous and it is located in Sydney." Edward added.

"And also Mom, we would be closer to home. I really have enjoyed being in the states with Grandma and Grandpa, but I miss you and Mark and being here. We all have so much fun."

Nancy had always been uneasy at change, and being so far from family was getting to be too much for her.

"We did apply for a scholarship there as well." Edward added. "And we will all be close Dad."

Smiling Mark and Emily hugged their children. "You both are pretty awesome."

Mark said. "If you don't get the scholarship I believe we can handle it."

Emily and Mark sort of expected them to want to come home and they were very happy about it. Soon they would all be together again. After Hank's schooling was complete they would be back too. Erika's plans were to come here after school too, but Emily wondered if she and Michael would stay together.

When the children went back to the states to finish school, Mark and Emily had a business trip to Melbourne and Sydney planned. A few new designs were ready to take to the directors of the new picture. Both of their businesses were doing well and so she and Mark had decided to buy some land in town by their little church in town. After their trip they would stop in town and see a realtor there.

"I am looking forward to this purchase." Mark said

"Me too. It is a nice piece of land and it has been empty for a long time." Emily agreed.

After the end of the transaction they went out to examine their purchase once more. "You know Mark," as she looked toward the little church, "the church really could use some repairs."

"I agree and I think Larry and the men and I should come in tomorrow and see what we can do."

"That would be nice and I am sure Pastor Sweeny will be grateful."

"Should we tell anyone about our purchase?"

"Not yet honey. When the time is right we will know."

Over the next few months the winter months came and went. September came with a beautiful spring day. After her quiet time Emily got up to join Mark in the kitchen for breakfast. A pain hit her about half way to the table. She stopped and looked at Mark who saw her face tighten. "Em, what's wrong?" He was out of his chair and by her side immediately. Then everything happened very fast, when she reached for Mark's hand she lost consciousness. Mark yelled for Kate to call the doctor and he picked her up and carried her up stairs. Pam and Becky came in with a cold cloth and put it on her forehead. Mark sat on the bed beside her. "Baby, don't leave me."

"Mark, I am fine. Please don't worry so."

"I know but I can't help myself right now."

"Mr. Mark, Kate said that Dr. Gordon is on his way, and to keep her still and comfortable until he arrives." Pam said.

It seemed like everything was happening at once. Her labor pains had started without warning and had intensified at an alarming rate. "Mark I don't think this baby is going to wait for Bob to get here. Tell Kate…" She paused as a pain took her breath away. She started her breathing techniques and then relaxed. Mark had already moved in behind her and was coaching her as they had learned in birthing classes. When the pain subsided, she continued, "Tell Kate to get water towels and blankets ready."

"I wish we had stayed in town." Mark actually didn't mean to say that aloud.

"We will be fine…" Another pain began and the breathing and the coaching started again.

"Kate!" Mark yelled out.

"Mark, Emily panted. I think it's coming now."

Kate entered with water and towels and the other ladies were there too. Mark positioned himself, ready to deliver the baby. After a few pushes the baby arrived. "It's a girl." Mark yelled about the time Bob walked in. He took over and the ladies took the baby and washed her then wrapped her in a blanket. Then they handed her to Mark who was talking softly to her as he examined his daughter. Mark was still worrying and at the same time marveling at the tiny little girl God had given them. She had a head full of dark black hair and delicate features like her mother. She was alert and wide eyed as she listened to Mark talking to her. He handed her to Emily to feed. Bob was telling them that the baby looked great and Emily's vital signs were good.

"Oh goodness Mark call Hank and Leigha." Emily insisted.

They called and Edward answered the phone. "Hi Dad, they left for the hospital a few minutes ago. I was just about to leave as soon as Nancy is ready."

"Well son, you two have a new baby sister."

"That's something Dad how did you know Leigha would be…No wait it was Emily wasn't it?" he laughed. "I will tell everyone and we will let you know as soon as our new arrival gets here."

Mark got off the phone and told them all that Edward had said. Emily said, "Their son will be here soon."

Everyone stopped and looked at her and Mark just shook his head at his wife's intuition.

"Well we can go to the states for graduation and Christmas." Emily laughed.

"Emily what are we going to name this little girl?" Mark asked.

"Anna Danielle Garrett." Emily said.

"Beautiful sweetheart." Mark agreed.

While they adored the baby and talking the phone rang. "Hey Dad we have a new son. We have named him Mark Alexander." Hank told him.

"Well we have Anna Danielle Garrett here." They talked for a few minutes assuring each other that the mothers and babies were fine.

The days passed and things were settling into a routine. Then they started planning their trip to the states. Emily had made gifts and shipped them ahead of time. Emily had forgotten how much she loved making little baby clothes. She made matching outfits for little Mark and Anna. She couldn't wait to see them together. Also seeing the older children graduate college was going to be the icing on the cake.

CHAPTER
FOURTEEN

Graduation day came and Emily and Mark were both so proud of their children. All of the future plans were becoming reality. Edward and Nancy surprised everyone by telling them,

"There is something we want to tell everyone while we are all together." Edward took Nancy's hand and said, "We eloped two weeks ago,"

"You know how I hate to be the center of attention, so I never really wanted a big wedding, Mom. I hope you aren't upset." Nancy added.

"Of course, I only want you to be happy." Emily hugged her daughter.

Then in the midst of everyone congratulating them, Michael drew Mark aside and asked. "Mr. Garrett, you know I have loved Erika for a long time. I would like your permission to marry your daughter."

Mark smiled at Michael and said, "Michael I am not really surprised. Of course and if she says yes then I gladly welcome you to the family."

All eyes turned toward Michael as he kneeled beside Erika, "Erika you know that I have loved you since we were kids. I will follow you to Australia, because I never want to be without you again. Will you marry me?" Erika smiled nodded yes as he placed a ring on her finger. Lynette and John were busy congratulating them.

Edward and Nancy announced to everyone, "We each received a scholarship to veterinary school in Sydney."

Erika smiled," I guess, it's our turn Michael. Michael, as you know, has received his family nurse practitioner license and I also have my RN license. Dr. Gordon had hired both of us to help at his clinic."

Mark stood up and asked, "Well Ariel, Wesley, and Louis what have you three to say?"

"Oh Dad," Wesley added, "We are going to be with you and Emily for many years."

Everyone laughed and patted him on the back.

"In fact, we never plan to get married and leave home." Ariel laughed.

"Don't look at me I plan to just take one day at a time. Maybe I will expand the old tree house and live in it." Louis teased. This had been a wonderful family time and Emily hated to see it end. Plans were made for a wedding for Michael and Erika in the near future. It was decided to have the wedding in Australia since Michael and Erika would be starting their jobs upon their return home. Michael would return to Australia with them and then Lynette and John would join them a few weeks before the wedding.

Larry and Kate even said they were looking forward to getting home, "Although we have loved the adventure we have had it will be nice to be home." Larry added.

Once again Emily tried to talk her Dad into moving to Australia and of course he said he was not old enough to retire. "Now, Emily you know that I have a few more messages to preach. God isn't through with me yet. Besides I need to be here for Hank. He, Leigha, and boys will be staying here in the garage apartment. I believe that God will use Hank in a big way so who better to mentor him than an old pastor." Samuel grinned at his daughter.

"You are right of course. And I think he will have a great mentor in you." Emily agreed.

God had blessed their family, Kate and Larry would be going back with them and would be helping Emily with baby Anna. Everything was falling into place. The trip home was uneventful and it was so good to be home. Now they had another wedding to plan for Michael and

Erika. This house had become home a place that at first had given her a sense of dread was now where she found refuge and comfort. Things had changed since the first day Emily had spent in Australia. All the events both sad and happy had led their lives to the place they were now. Emily had lost Alex; Mark had lost Robyn; and they both had lost a baby. Yet, through it all Emily and Mark had found each other, and God had blessed them with a baby. Although losing Robyn and Alex had devastated them, they had found strength in God's eternal love.

Sometimes Emily thought about Alex's death and she often wondered why in spite of her warnings from her visions and even after both Alex and Mark had the visions, Alex had chosen to drive in the storm. He had always listened to her warnings before and he had believed her past premonitions. Yet, that night when every condition was the same as her dream had been, but because of his love and worry about her being alone he had chosen to ignore it all. Even though she understood now that it was all part of God's perfect plan, it was still hard to bear at times. Through it all she had learned that to know God's will, she had to be willing to let Him lead and put her will and what she wanted out of life aside and let God and His will be her will.

When Robyn died, first Mark was bitter, but he renewed his faith by turning to God. He studied God's Word daily and learned from it. Mark was such an inspiration to her and everyone by showing how God can help us overcome sorrow and loss. He always seemed to know what to do and what scriptures to use to help.

Through all of the pain of her loss, Mark had become her strong shoulder to lean on when Alex died. Looking back at everything she realized that it was Mark that helped her remember that God was always with her. It was Mark who was there to help her and it was Mark who had lifted her away from Alex's dead body. It was Mark who had rescued her after her accident. He was the one who kept her alive and brought her back from the brink of death through his persistence. Now he was a part of her heart forever.

Now sitting here she had remembered the past. Yes, she was comfortable with the changes that she had gone through. Had she known all that would happen would she still have made the decision to come here? She nodded her head because she knew that because of these things she was closer to God and He had blessed her life in so many ways.

Mark was watching her as she smiled and nodded her head as if she was answering a question in the affirmative. Moving up behind her he placed his hands on her shoulders.

"A penny for your thoughts," a familiar voice from behind her brought her back from her thoughts.

"Just a penny?" She replied as she turned to face Mark.

"Well if you give me a tell, then I will decide if there is more in it for you." He was now standing in front of her.

"Oh, really? Well I was thinking about you." She grinned. "What's it worth to you, now?"

"Well, I am a very interesting subject-in fact there is only one subject I like better."

"Oh I see. What subject would that be, my good man."

Mark reached out and lifted her in his arms and kissed her. Then Emily leaned back and said, "So, your favorite subject is kissing?"

"Good guess. Well there is something else I find interesting, and it is another interesting subject." Emily laughed as Mark raised his eyebrows and with his eyes motioned to the stairs.

"I already knew that one." She and they smiled at each other then turned to watch the sunrise. This man was her happiness and through all their losses they had found each other. She knew that it had been God's plan and because of her dream the night of her accident she knew that both Alex and Robyn were pleased that they had found each other. As they stood facing the new day, Mark put his arms around her.

"Sweetheart, that old saying 'When God closes a door, He opens a window' has certainly been true in our lives," Mark said holding her close.

"I believe that too." Then together they both said, "God doesn't make mistakes!"

And somewhere out there Alex and Robyn joined in the sentiment.

ABOUT THE AUTHOR

Recia McLeod Edmonson is a retired English teacher. Realizing that many times people will chose reading a fiction book over nonfiction or the Bible, she wrote this book. It is full of Biblical truths as well as a good story about how God can work in people's lives. Recia lost her husband of thirty-nine years to cancer and after losing his battle with cancer he left this world to take up residence in his heavenly home.

The journey to have this work published was one that was met with much prayer and seeking God's will. Her main goal for this book is that God will use it for His honor and glory.

It is fiction, but it also holds the truth of God's will and control in people's lives. Her beloved husband, David inspired the book with his comment "God doesn't make mistakes."

Printed in the United States
By Bookmasters